What readers

The Nash Sisters . . . is a treasu_____ _____ginal story told with an authentic voice. Strong women characters seem genuine and their story, woven against the backdrop of historical events and real places, is compelling. I highly recommend the book and look forward to more from the author.

— *Stefanie Mendell*

I feel as though I have four new friends: the Nash sisters. Reading about the Nash Sisters brought back wonderful memories of my mother and her sisters. I loved reading stories from the different voices of each sister. What a wonderful idea to have a Round-Robin letter and great concept for us today using email. I think the cover is perfect for the focus of the book.

— *Susan Bloom*

The Nash Sisters is a heart-warming story about family and life. The events that the characters [experience] are relatable, despite the fact they take place in the '20s, '30s and '40s. I found myself getting drawn into each of their stories and couldn't put the book down. I look forward to learning more about their stories [in the] next novel(s).

— *Angella Schroller*

The Nash Sisters is a great book! I really liked how it flowed. Getting the perspective of each sister is done in creative and unique ways. . . . I can't wait for the next Nash Sisters book!

— *Monica Carolin*

Happiness Doesn't Come Easy

A Nash Sisters Novel

Happiness
Doesn't
Come Easy

A Nash Sisters Novel

Leatha Marie

• WRITE WAY •
PUBLISHING COMPANY
RALEIGH, NORTH CAROLINA

Printed in the United States of America
ISBN 978-1-946425-85-0

Book Design by CSinclaire Write-Design
Cover Design by Klevur

• WRITE WAY •
PUBLISHING COMPANY
RALEIGH, NORTH CAROLINA

Books by Leatha Marie

The Nash Sisters

A heart-warming novel introducing four sisters
growing up in the rural South in the
1920s, 1930s, and 1940s

Happiness Doesn't Come Easily

Life brings hardship, joy, and new beginnings
to the Nash Sisters, and through it all,
family love and support are always there.

Thank you to my readers who tell me
to keep writing and to my family who remind me
that a book takes time to develop.

Happiness Doesn't Come Easy

The Nash sisters, Ethel, Annie, and Caroline, are back!

Though the timeline for this story spans less than two years, it is a time that brings many changes to the sisters and to the world around them. The Nash sisters, and all those who have joined the family, dodge the twists and turns of life without forgetting to notice the happiness within. A lesson for all of us.

Contents

CHAPTER 1 — AUGUST 1945

Ethel
Bombs Bursting in Air

I HATE TELEPHONES. THEY EXPECT you to stop what you're doing and come running when they ring.

I was in the back of the house sorting the laundry of people I don't know. But they pay me, so that is more important than the dang telephone. It would not stop ringing—6, 7, 8, 9 rings. Oh SUGAR, I may as well get it!

I had taken off my sandals and rushed to the front of the house in my socks. I nearly tripped over the step that divides the laundry business from the kitchen. "Alright, alright, I'm coming," I shouted to no one. When I picked up the earpiece, I heard crying. It was one of my sisters, but I couldn't make out which one.

"Hello. Who is this? Hello. I can't understand what you are saying. Settle down so I can hear you!" I was screaming to be heard over the hysterics.

"Ethel, Ethel something terrible has happened!" the

voice said. "Oh, what are we going to do? The bombs are going to kill us all. We're all going to die. It is just horrible!"

I was getting as upset as the caller. What could be so terrible, I thought? "Caroline, is that you? Where are you? Is someone there with you? Calm down and tell me what has happened!"

Then the call went dead. I stood stunned and scared. The earpiece dropped from my hand and dangled from the table to the floor. My body was rigid. It was like rigor mortis had struck me.

Larry came running into the kitchen from outside, shouting, "Ethel, what is it? Ethel, are you okay?"

I could not move. I could not speak. I could not breathe. Larry clutched my shoulder and leaned toward me. My head fell against his chest. "Breathe, baby girl, breathe slowly," he said. "What has happened? Who was that on the telephone?"

Then I felt my body become fluid. My jelly legs couldn't hold me. Larry was quick enough to pull the kitchen chair under me before I fell to the floor. He grabbed the earpiece to the telephone trying to revive the call. "Hello, hello. Who's there?" He began tapping the button where the earpiece sits. Nothing there. Then he hung it up.

He grabbed my shoulders again, but this time he shook me. Then I heard him. His voice was strong. I looked up at his face. "Ethel, you're okay. I'm here. I'll bring you some water or something stronger, but you have to tell me what happened."

"I need some Jack! Water won't help," I said, almost

yelling at him. Stupid man, I thought. Can't he tell I need a drink!

He handed me the small glass of the brown liquid, and I downed it quickly. It took a minute to stop the burn in my throat, but it helped get my wits about me.

"I'm not sure who that was on the telephone, but I think it was Caroline. She sounded terrified—crying and screaming about something terrible happening to her, and then the line when dead. I have to call her back. Get me the address book. I'll call Belle Parker at Dix Hospital. I don't have the number at the house where Caroline lives now. Someone needs to get to her!"

~~~

Caroline is my youngest sister and the most fragile. When she was a teenager, she was burned in a fire and taken to the hospital for her medical care. Then, to help her mental state, they moved her to Dorothea Dix State Hospital for the Insane in Raleigh. Caroline lived there until just recently. Now she lives with a family, taking care of two children and keeping house. We talk as much as we can, and I write every now and then when I can't visit. Caroline still has moments of craziness, but mostly she's better. I can't figure out what got her so upset. I have to find someone at the hospital to go check on her.

Annie is my other sister. She lives in Washington, DC, with her husband and two young children. I'll call Annie as soon as I get this sorted out. No need to scare her to death like Caroline did me.

Larry was rummaging around in the kitchen

cabinets looking for my telephone number book. I was mad that he was making a mess of things, so I took a minute to think. Yep, I knew where it was. I pulled out the drawer under the kitchen table, and there it was. With my bossy tone I said, "I got it. Stop tearing up the place."

Turning the pages, I got to the entry I had made for Dix Hill. I had written right beside it "crazy hospital in Raleigh." Well, that was stupid. Like I'd ever forget that place. I went to the telephone, picked up the earpiece, and tapped the button until the operator picked up and said, "Number please." I told her the number. It only rang once before someone answered. Thank God.

I wasn't clear myself about what I wanted, so I just started talking. "Is there anything going on there? My sister used to live there and now she lives with a family. She just called me having a crazy fit, but she couldn't tell me what was wrong. I don't know how to reach the family she lives with, and I live in Burlington and can't run right over there. My sister, Caroline Nash, acted like someone was out to get her. She said something about a bomb. Then the telephone cut off. I am nuts with worry. Can you get me Belle Parker? She knows me and my sister. In fact, Caroline lives with Belle's son and daughter-in-law. I think the neighborhood is called Oakwood or something."

Larry was leaning close to me and the telephone. I guess he could hear the person on the other line wasn't talking. He took the telephone from my hand, put his pointer finger up to his lips and said to me "Shhh . . ." Any other time he wouldn't have got away with shushing me, but I needed his help to make this woman understand.

He spoke calmly into the telephone, "Ma'am, this is Larry Martin. I am calling for Ethel Martin. Maybe I can help you understand what Ethel needs. Is it okay if I tell you what she wants?"

I heard a muffled voice say, "Of course. That would be helpful, Mr. Martin."

"Ethel needs to speak with Belle Parker. Mrs. Parker works at Dix Hill. Do you know her?"

The operator said, "I'm afraid I do not. There are many people working here. What is her position? Or what doctor does she work with?"

I blurted out loud enough for the lady to hear me, "Doctor Redmond. Dr. Tom Redmond. Belle works with his patients!"

"Okay, I will transfer this call to Dr. Redmond's office. His secretary will be able to help."

I got stiff, scared the line would drop once again. Every minute passing might be too late for Caroline.

Larry held the earpiece away from his ear and leaned toward me so I could hear. In just a few rings, I could hear a voice on the line, "Dr. Redmond's office. How can I help?"

Larry repeated what he said before, but he was talking too slow, so I grabbed the earpiece from him. I knew I better get to the point. "This is Ethel Nash. I mean Ethel Nash Fox Martin. My sister Caroline Nash is a patient of Dr. Redmond, and she's in a terrible way. She called me in a hissy fit, crying and screaming. She said something terrible happened. I need to call

Belle Parker but don't have her number. Can you give it to me?" By this time my forehead was all sweaty. My legs felt like jelly again, so I plopped back down on the chair.

In a firm but comforting voice, the woman said, "Mrs. Martin, it will be fine. I know Miss Caroline Nash. We will get her the help that she needs. Give me your telephone number in case the line clicks off. I will put the telephone down and go promptly to Dr. Redmond."

I gave her my number, and in the silence, I began to breathe more slowly. Larry put his arm around my shoulders. Sweet man. He's always solid like that when I need it. It seemed like an eternity, but by my watch she was only gone for 10 minutes. When she came back to the line, she said, "Mrs. Martin, Dr. Redmond will have someone go pick up Caroline and bring her here. I am to contact Mrs. Belle Parker and make sure she can meet them there. It might take some time, but a nurse will go in the car to give Caroline what she needs right away. You may have Mrs. Parker's phone number for future reference, but Dr. Redmond suggests you not call her now. He has a plan to get Caroline safe and that includes Mrs. Parker. Is that okay with you?"

I began to cry softly, not like a lunatic. I can cry that way too. This was a relief kind of cry. Through the tears I replied, "Yes ma'am. That's okay. That's just fine. Will the doctor call as soon as he knows what might be happening? Please."

"Yes. We will ring you back at the number I have as soon as we can. Please be patient. It might take a few hours. Dr. Redmond wants you to know that Caroline will be treated right away. He asked me to tell you that we know Caroline and will welcome her back. Is someone with you, Mrs. Martin?"

"Yes. My Larry is with me. I will begin packing some things to drive to Raleigh. He can drive me. But I'll wait to hear back from y'all. I need to call my other sister."

"Okay, very good," said the voice of an angel from heaven.

"Ma'am, what is your name? You've been really nice."

"Mrs. Martin, I am Teresa Mills, Dr. Redmond's secretary. My direct line is TE 4329. If you have not heard from us in an hour or so, you can ring me."

Reluctantly, I hung up the telephone.

Larry was trying to reassure me. "Ethel, it'll be all right. From what you tell me about these people, they took care of Caroline at her worst. They are the best ones to be in charge now."

I knew he was right, and I loved him for saying that. I am so glad I married this man. He's so good. My little sister, Annie, said one time, "If you don't tie the knot, he will get away."

After a cup of coffee with a little helper added from the liquor cabinet, I was feeling better. I grabbed the telephone and asked the operator to ring me Annie's number. I knew that number by heart.

The telephone rang only two times. Annie must have been close to the telephone. "Cheerio! This is Annie!" she said in her cheerful voice.

"Annie, it's Ethel. Do you have time to talk? Are the children settled where they won't be able to hear?"

"Yes, of course I have time to talk, dear sister. I have been thinking about you all day. Did you hear about the nuclear bomb that the US dropped on Japan? I wanted to talk to you about it. It seems terrible! The children are with Lelia. We can talk."

I was irritated that she began talking from the beginning. But she always does that. She doesn't want to waste a minute. "I haven't heard about a bomb in Japan. You can tell me about that later. I'm calling to talk to you about Caroline. She had a spell and Dr. Redmond from Dix Hill is sending people over to get her and bring her to the hospital."

Now I had her attention. "Oh no! Is she okay? What happened? Did someone do something to her? Tell me everything."

I told her the details of what happened the last few hours. I even told her how nice the secretary was, how Dr. Redmond was taking charge, and that Larry was with me every minute. "I don't know what happened to Caroline, but it must have been really bad. She's been so much better living with the Parkers. The last few times we talked I got the feeling that she knows the work is good for her. And the children seem to really like her. Isn't that how it seems to you when y'all talk?"

"Yes. And the independence is good for her! Remember our last visit? She went on and on about feeling normal and independent. She even made a few comments about the money rolling in."

I snickered. That's what I needed—laughter. Nash sisters' laughter. "Yeah, and she said Mr. Parker offered her a raise, and she took it. But she said she didn't know what to do with so much money. She said she might buy a car!"

We were both giggling now. I think the whiskey was taking hold on me.

Annie spit out a laugh and said, "Yes, good God. She said she might buy my old green Ambassador! You said that was nonsense since she didn't even know how to drive. Her answer was she didn't need to drive it. She just wanted to park it on the street!"

A quiet moment came between us. Although it felt good to talk about the happy times, we knew there was a cloud of sadness around us. I repeated the words we've used since we were young. "Annie, it is a sad/happy time."

Almost in a whisper, Annie said, "It sure is."

"Annie, I need to hang up so the telephone line is open when they call me back. I will ring you back after you put Lisa and Jon Jr. to bed. Or does Lelia do that while you kick back and drink coffee." I was trying to keep the mood light.

"I put them to bed when I can, but Lelia is always there as my backup. I might get it wrong," she chuckled. "Okay, sister, please call me as soon as you can."

"Hey you," I said. "It's good to talk with you, Annie. I needed to hear your voice. And we can talk about the bomb later."

I could hear a smile behind the voice. "The bomb seems really unimportant right now, Ethel. Only family matters right this minute. Love you, girlie," which was the way Annie always signed off from a call.

~~~

As I waited at the table by the phone, I tried to read the newspaper. I fidgeted with my coffee, then went to find the box where I kept the Nash Round-Robin Letters. I quickly found a box that caused memories to flood my brain. It was the HAV-A-TAMPA box that our oldest sister, Dianne, used for her important papers. I opened the lid and saw the picture of one of the prettiest ladies I'd ever seen. She looked different to me now. I remember her wearing a beautiful blue dress. But her style is more elegant than a child would notice. Her dress has a green bodice and one sleeve slung low on her shoulder. There was a long purple skirt draped around her. The fabric clung to her. I flashed to the gold sash tied around her hips. I can't believe I missed all this classiness before. I still think she looks like a Nash sister.

There was that day. I could see my 12-year-old Marie holding my dear George's hand. Dianne was lying on the bed with her 10-year-old Suzy sitting beside her. We were quiet, watching Dianne give up living. The contents of the box changed our lives. It held the papers that allowed us to bring Suzy into our family to be Marie's sister. The official adoption papers were in there, all worked out by Dianne and my George before Dianne got really sick. I closed the lid and held the box to my chest. I missed my big sister so much. I wanted her here today to help us with Caroline. I heard Larry's footsteps and dried up my tears.

"Anything new on Caroline, sugar?" He called me sugar when he wanted to be sweet. But he also used the word as a cuss word. I wished he would pick a new sweet word for me.

"Nothing yet," I said. "I talked to Annie and told her what I know. Funny thing is she started the call talking about a bomb in Japan. Caroline mentioned a bomb in her craziness. Do you know anything about a bomb?" Even though I didn't want something else to worry about, I was curious why it came up twice this afternoon.

Larry sat down at the kitchen table with me and put his hands on mine. He said, "Yeah, it has been on the radio and in the newspaper. The American military dropped two atomic bombs on Japanese cities. It was in retaliation for Japan's attack on Pearl Harbor. They say over a hundred thousand people died immediately. It's terrible, Ethel. I don't know how you missed that news, but I didn't bring it up. I didn't want to talk about it. I can't imagine why President Harry Truman would do such a thing. The radio news guys say it was his attempt to end the world war. I think it is way too horrible. You want to listen to the radio and find out more?"

I pulled my hands out from under Larry's and pushed both hands deep in the pockets of my dress. "Oh good God NO! I can't handle anything more right now. If Caroline heard about this, no wonder she's in a fit. She still has a hard time getting things straight about what's here and now and what's not real at all. Does the news say whether Japan will bomb us back? Are we in danger?"

Then I changed my mind about talking about this.

"Never mind. I don't want to know anything more. I can't think about this right now."

To get my mind off the fact that I'd not heard from Dr. Redmond, I went back to searching for the box where I keep the Nash Round-Robin Letters. As I pulled the dust-covered box from under our bed, my heart began to swell. Not only because of the letters in there but because the box reminds me of Momma. It's wooden and has faded print on the side that says:

MAGIC .EAST MAKES GOOD BREAD

The words were smeared and worn away by many hands over many years. Momma could recall words printed on the box every time we brought it down to get bags of flour, salt, yeast, and other baking goods that were stored there. All the time we lived in Momma's house, my sisters and I saw that box on top of the Hoosier cabinet in the kitchen. When Dianne and I were very young, we would make up the missing letters. We named it Magic East brand because we thought anything made in the eastern part of the world must be magical.

MAGIC EAST MAKES GOOD BREAD even when Dianne makes it. (Or Ethel if Dianne is saying it.)

MAGIC EAST MAKES GOOD BREAD for the boys that come to visit—'cause that is the only way a boy will come visit the Nash sisters.

MAGIC EAST MAKES GOOD BREAD for your magic powers.

MAGIC EAST MAKES GOOD BREAD even when it goes bad, cause the pigs like it.

As I moved my hands into the box and felt the worn, handwritten papers, my mind brought me back to where I was. Away from those memories in Momma's kitchen, back to mine. Now that we have a telephone, we don't write so much. I hate that. Because getting a Nash Round-Robin Letter is like a present, a permanent history of our lives. I ended up with the sets from everyone because when Dianne died, I got hers. Annie knew I would be better at keeping things, so she sent me her letters last year. Caroline really couldn't keep things where she lived, so I brought them here. I had to put them in Momma's Magic Yeast box because there are so many of them.

I read the first letters we wrote to each other. They were funny, terrifying, and sweet. It showed how good we were to each other. I'm glad we have these.

I'll get another round-robin started after we get all this figured out with Caroline. I think I'll add Marie and Suzy to the letters. They're old enough to tell us about their lives. I'll probably have to give them postage money.

On top of the stack was the first letter I had written to my sisters. It had the instructions on how the round-robin would work. Of course, I wrote the rules. Me bossing my sisters around was necessary. We would never get this right if I didn't take charge. And if we didn't follow the directions, it would cost too much to mail. None of us had much money back then. This is how it started.

Instructions for the Nash Round-Robin Letters
March 5, 1930

We talked about this when you were last home, but in case you don't remember the details, here is what was decided.

Add a letter to the round-robin letters each time the envelope comes around. I hope we can have the robin go 'round at least once a month. Don't hold the letters more than a few days before mailing them. Even if you are busy or can't think of anything to say, just make comments on what other letters have said. You can write letters front and back and no more than two sheets of paper to save on postal costs. Here is the way the Nash Round-Robin Letters will go. I'll start it since it was my idea. I write my letter and mail it to Dianne. Dianne, you write to us about your life in Burlington and mail my letter and yours to Caroline. Since we are never sure where Caroline will be living next, she has asked the postmaster to hold her mail. She promised to save some money for stamps and go pick up her mail once a week. Caroline, please write your letter as soon as you can, add it to letters from Dianne and me then send all of them to Annie. Annie, you contribute your letter and send all four back to me. I know you have a Roaring Twenties life to tell us all about, but please try to keep to two sheets of paper. When I get the letter from Annie, we have completed one round-robin. I take out my letter and start it all over again with a new letter.

When the telephone rang, I just about jumped out of my skin! I picked up the telephone earpiece and shoved it to the side of my head so hard that it nearly knocked me out. Larry came running from the back of the house, tripping over the step up to the kitchen.

"Hello, hello," I said quickly. "This is Ethel Nash Fox Martin, who is this?"

The voice on the line was clear as day. "Ethel, it's Caroline. They let me call you. I'm okay. I went crazy for a bit, but the nurse gave me lots of medicine. I am okay. I won't be able to talk long because their high-powered medicine knocks me out pretty quick. I just wanted to call and tell you I'm okay."

I was trying to be calm and not upset Caroline, but everybody knows I am not good at being calm. "Oh, Caroline, it's good to hear your voice. You scared the bajeebies out of me! I'm glad you're okay. Where are you? What happened?"

I could tell the medicine was calming Caroline. Her voice was only a little agitated. "It was the bombs, Ethel. The radio said they landed in Japan, but I don't know how far away that is. I heard the bombs from the Parkers' house and knew they were really close. I grabbed the children and ran to the basement. The bombs were dropping all around. I knew we were going to die. The Parkers have a telephone in the base-ment, so I called you. But the phone went dead. The bombs had hit in Oakwood."

I was pacing as far as the telephone cord would let me go. Holding it together was not easy. She was making no sense. "Caroline, listen to me. There aren't any bombs being dropped in Raleigh, North Carolina! Japan is on the other side of the world. Where are you now? Are the nurses with you?"

Caroline's speech was slurring and turning into a whisper. "Ethel, I heard the bombs. If I can hear them, they are close by. Now I'm at Dix Hill. They told me they have a bomb shelter, and I'll be safe here. I'm gonna take a nap. I am gonna be okay. The children and I are safe here."

There was a long pause on the line. Then someone else spoke, "Mrs. Martin? This is Joanna Dunn. I'm here with Caroline. She's falling asleep. That is the best thing for her. I'll pull the telephone out of her room so you and I can talk."

There was shuffling in the background. I just didn't want the telephone to hang up. No telling how long it would take to get back to them. As I was pacing, Larry stood ready with his hands on the back of the chair. He was set to move the chair wherever I was when my legs went jelly again.

Joanna's voice came back on the line. "Mrs. Nash, I mean Mrs. Martin. Joanna Dunn here. May I call you Ethel?"

"Yes, please do. Nobody knows which last name I'm using anyway. You wouldn't believe how many last names I really have," I replied.

"Let me tell you what I know so far about Caroline. We will not know everything for a couple of days.

Please understand that Caroline is indeed safe here. I'm not talking about safe from bombs. I'm talking about her mental health. We will take very good care of her. I was with the team that went to the Parkers' house to pick up Caroline and make sure the children were safe. Belle Parker was also with us and two male assistants. Belle had a key and was able to get us into the house. I assume you know the family that Caroline lives with is Belle's son's family."

"Yes. Belle is so dear to Caroline. I'm glad Belle was there."

"Once we were in the house, Belle called out to Caroline. The children called back to their grandma from the basement of the house. Caroline screamed for them to stay quiet. She was telling the children that someone was coming to bomb the house and that they were only safe in the basement. Both children were crying and calling for their grandma. The two male assistants raced to the basement door and shoved their shoulder into it. The door broke free from its lock, and it flung open. Belle rushed down the stairs, grabbed the little ones and bent down to hold them tight. I ran to Caroline telling her we were here and that she was safe. Caroline began shaking and crying uncontrollably. She fell to the floor in violent seizures. We grabbed laundry to put under and around her so she would not injure herself. While the men held her down, I injected a sedative. Her body began to calm."

I felt grateful but really worried. "Joanna, thank you for taking care of Caroline. I know she was terrified. When she was very young and feeling anxious her body would shake until I or someone could calm her down. I've never seen her have the kind of violent shakes you are talking about. Poor Caroline."

Nearly whispering, Joanna said, "Caroline will stay in the hospital unit for several days, maybe longer."

I planned out loud as tears began to spill down my cheeks. "Me and my husband will come to Raleigh and see her. I want to talk to Belle and make sure the children are okay. I hope Caroline did not harm them in any way."

The nurse was silent for a moment then reassured me, "Ethel, you are certainly welcome to come and talk with Dr. Redmond. I doubt Caroline will be able to see you until she has stabilized."

I was in a full-blown cry now. I put the earpiece on the table, laid my head down and sobbed into the gingham table cloth. Larry took the earpiece and said goodbye for me. Or at least that is what I think he did. I could not hear over my wailing.

CHAPTER 2

Annie
Southern Prejudice Coming to Light

I CALLED ETHEL SEVERAL TIMES, but there was no answer. It's not like her not to pick up the telephone. She likes talking. And this time, especially, we needed to talk so she could tell me how Caroline is doing. And if Ethel couldn't answer, Larry sure would. All I could do is pace around the living room near the telephone so I could hear it ring. I was a nervous wreck. I began to plan what to do next. I needed to go to Raleigh. I needed to talk to Jon. I needed to put my arms around my sisters.

Not realizing I had been pacing for hours, I jumped when the front door opened. "Hello, Annie, I'm home! Sorry I am late. What a day!" It was Jon's voice. I went running to the front of the house and jumped into his arms. He dropped his satchel and swept me up and spun me around, "Well, I am happy to see you too! That's the kind of welcome a man likes to get—an eager beaver."

I pushed myself back from him once my feet landed on the floor. He got a good look at my face. "Oh darling, you've been crying. What's going on? I completely got the wrong idea." Then his strong arms brought me back to him. As my head landed on his chest, the tears began gushing.

Without breathing between thoughts, I started rattling off what Ethel had told me. "Jon, something terrible has happened to Caroline! Ethel called to tell me they are taking her back to Dix Hill Hospital. She's gone psychotic again, and none of us are with her. She has terrified those sweet children she cares for. She told Ethel that the Japanese are dropping bombs in Raleigh. Ethel said she would call me back after the hospital staff picked up Caroline. She was going to talk to Dr. Redmond as soon as he knew something. That was hours ago. I have heard nothing. I have called Ethel and Larry three times and they don't answer the telephone. I don't know what is going on, and I am petrified! I don't know what to do! I must be here for the children. But I also need to go to Raleigh."

Jon began to smooth my hair. The movement was soft and rhythmic. I felt his chest moving in and out and heard his breathing. It was calm and relaxed. His ability to be composed even when everything around him is chaotic is such a gift. Thank goodness because that is what I needed right now.

He said, "Annie, together we can figure this out. We can do this. I am here now; we can solve this problem together." He continued to run his fingers through my hair, pushing it back from my face and turning it under at the bottom. He flattened the areas that I had twisted with my hair raking, a nervous habit I cannot seem to break.

He calms me like a glass of strong whiskey—only better. Jon brought me over to the couch, sat down beside me, and said, "Let's think this through."

I was sniffling but calming down. I thought quickly of Momma saying to us girls when we would get out of hand, "Alright girls, now is the time to be calm, cool, and collected." I miss my momma.

I nodded my head. Jon began to take charge. "It's late, so we can't do much tonight. I can make a call to get an update from the hospital on Caroline. Ethel probably forgot to call you and went to bed. Or they jumped in the car and went to Raleigh. Either way it was inconsiderate of her not to call you. You can indeed go to Raleigh or go to Burlington to see Ethel. We can figure out how and when to get you there. Lelia and I can handle the children. Or Lelia can go with you and you take the children. Whatever you want to do, we can make it happen. I don't think either of us can make anything happen tonight. It's nearly midnight. We need to get some sleep. We can learn more in the morning. Tomorrow you might call your friend Jane Hines. She still teaches nursing at Dix Hill, correct?"

What a relief. Movement was happening toward knowing what to do. "Yes, she does. You're right, she can find out about Caroline. I don't know why I didn't think of that."

We got up from the couch, and he guided me to

the bedroom. As we walked by the wine cabinet, he grabbed one of the special bottles of red wine. "I'll be back in a moment. I'm going to kiss my children. Then we can get ready for bed, soothe our minds with Mouton Rothschild, and you can tell me all about what the Nash sisters might do in this situation. You guys will be just fine." I smiled because he was echoing what my family said to each other when times were difficult.

I must have fallen right to sleep. I don't remember finishing my glass of wine or even talking to Jon. The next thing I knew the sun was peeking through the draperies and I could hear Jon's voice in the other room talking to someone on the telephone. I jumped out of bed, gathering my robe and slippers as I headed toward his voice. Jon smiled broadly and pointed to the kitchen and then to the earpiece of the telephone. My slippers swished on the floor as I nearly ran across the room when I heard him say, "Yes, Ethel, she's up now and dashing to the other telephone."

Our second telephone is in the kitchen. As I rounded the corner into the kitchen, I almost lost my footing but grabbed the telephone receiver to steady myself. Obviously, slippers are not good running shoes.

"Hello! Hello! Ethel, is that you?" Even before she could answer, I shouted, "Why didn't you call me back last night? I was worried sick! Jon had to put me in a wine stupor to calm me down!"

Ethel was defensive. "Don't you go getting smart with me, little sister. I have had a heck of a bad 24 hours. I am glad you got some sleep because I haven't slept a wink, lady. Shut it and let me explain!"

Boy, that sounded like Momma when she got really mad. So, I shut up. At that I heard Jon hang up the other telephone. He certainly didn't want to be a part of Ethel's ranting and raving.

"Annie, it took forever for them to call me from the hospital. I wasted time waiting. Larry and I could have gotten to Raleigh quicker than that. But finally, Joanna called. You remember her. She was the nurse assigned to Caroline in the last few months before Caroline left the asylum. Nurse Joanna has red hair like Maureen O'Hara. Caroline liked her, so I trusted what she had to say."

I could hear trembling in my sister's voice like when we have to talk in front of a group or to someone really important. Trying to bring the panic down, I took a deep breath and said, "Ethel, slow down and just hit the high points. You can tell me all the details later. Is Caroline okay? Are the children safe?"

As if copying me, I heard Ethel breathe deeply. In my mind, I could see her raising her head to breathe in, dropping it before she breathed out. We have done this since we were children. In the beginning it was a way to calm Caroline. Soon we learned this technique helped us all.

"Annie, I'm worried. Really worried. They had to handcuff Caroline to get her out of the basement and bring her to the hospital. Joanna gave her some heavy-duty drugs that kept her from harming herself or anybody. The good thing is I got to speak to Caroline. She was a mess and still believed there were bombs going off. She said she was in the hospital's bomb shelter now. Caroline's story was different from Joanna's. After Caroline fell asleep, Joanna took the telephone and told me more details. I'll give you the high points. The children are okay, and Caroline is in the doctor's hands. Larry and I are in Raleigh staying at a guest cottage on the Dix Hill property."

When Ethel is "worried, really worried," then all hell has broken lose. She was glossing over it for me. I must get to Raleigh.

"Oh my word, Ethel. It sounds terrible. I don't want you to handle this all by yourself. You have had to do so much of that in our life. I will come down today. The drive should get me there late this afternoon. Tell me the telephone number where you are and I will call as soon as I get in town. Jon can't get away from his job with all that is going on at the Pentagon. I might bring the children and Lelia. How does that sound?"

"That would be grand!" Ethel said. "I'm not sure where all of us can stay. Marie is coming over at lunchtime. She's hoping we can see Caroline then. I am not so sure we'll be able to."

Ethel gave me a telephone number. I wrote it a second time on another sheet of paper to leave for Jon. I figured Ethel would not be at this number much of the day. She would be organizing things, doing her detective work, and most likely visiting Belle. My hand began twirling my hair as I began to line up what needed to be done. Using Jon's words to comfort us both I said, "We can figure all this out together." Then I heard the click of the call ending.

Jane Hines was a woman I met right after

moving to DC. She and I had much in common, but I didn't know how important she would become to our family. Jane now lives in Raleigh and is teaching nurses at Dorothea Dix State Mental Hospital. She has been so helpful with our family's understanding of what Caroline's illness can do to her behaviors. I picked up the telephone receiver, tapped the button to reach an operator, and gave her Jane's telephone number at home. It was too early for Jane to be at work. After two rings, there was Jane's voice. Just hearing it made me tear up.

As I spoke, my voice cracked. "Jane, this is Annie Nash Walsh. I am sorry to call so early, but I need to talk to you about my sister, Caroline."

She responded with kind happiness, "Oh Annie, it is so good to hear from you. We don't talk nearly enough. Caroline? I haven't seen her in a long time. How is she doing in her job with the Parker family?"

"Jane, Caroline has had a relapse. She believes there are bombs hitting Raleigh, and she is the only one that can keep the Parker children safe. They have taken her back to Dix. Can you do me a great favor and check on her? She was admitted yesterday. My sister Ethel is in Raleigh, and I will be there before the evening. I know this is asking a lot, but we need your help—again."

Switching from friend Jane, she responded in her professional manner. "Of course, Annie. I will see what I can find out. Who is the attending physician? Dr. Redmond?"

I began feeling more in control. I was able to

get some help for us, Caroline's sisters. "Yes, Jane, Dr. Redmond. And the nurse who went to the Parker's house to transport Caroline is Joanna Dunn."

"Okay, Annie, I have lots of questions, but you should get started on your trip to Raleigh. If you give me your permission, I can get answers from Nurse Dunn. Call me again when you arrive in Raleigh. I should be home about six."

With a big sigh of relief, I said, "Of course you have my permission. You might be able to see Ethel before I get there. She'll give you any permission you need. Thank you, Jane."

It is amazing how quickly sadness can move to happiness with a few words. It used to be common in our family to have happy/sad and sad/happy moments at the same time. When you know that, you know things will be okay.

I went to tell Jon and Lelia about my plans. Lelia had arrived to begin her day with me and the family. Jon was talking quietly to her as I entered the living room. "Jon, I would like to take the children with me to Raleigh. I don't know how long I will need to stay. Lelia, can you go with me? I will need a smart and organized companion. I am not sure I can think straight about all that needs to be done."

Lelia smiled and looked at Jon. Jon said with a little smirk, "I think I could be an organized companion, but smart? Lelia is better at both of those traits. She is also very flexible. Right, Lelia?"

And there he was again. Saying just the right thing for both of us.

Lelia replied, "Miss Walsh, I can do whatever you need. Mr. Walsh was just telling me that your sister is not well, and she needs you. And, of course, your babies need to be with their momma. Anything I can do, I will. You know how I love those young'uns." Lelia leaned a bit to one side, put her hands on her hips and added, "I'll call my momma right away and tell her I am traveling to Raleigh. Oh lawd! She will flip her wig over this! Her youngest is going to North Carolina!"

Jon and I both laughed. I adore this beautiful Negro woman. Only Lelia could bring excitement to misfortune. She brings such fun to our house—and smarts!

Jon wanted to contribute, "Okay, lovely ladies, go tell the children about this adventure. Get yourselves packed, and so you don't have to worry about driving, I will arrange train tickets and a hotel in Raleigh. I know just the right place. Annie, should I get a room for Larry and Ethel and Marie and Suzy too?"

"Yes, please. This will be an adventure for sure! Thank you, Lelia, I couldn't do this without you."

I let Lelia tell the children. She nearly ran into their room, plopped down on the overstuffed chair and pulled them into her lap. "Okay, Lisa. Now listen, little Jon. Your momma and me are takin' you on a train ride. We're goin' to Raleigh to see family. If you both mind your manners, I'll take you to see some things you never saw before. Remember that story about Curious George going on an adventure with the man in the yellow hat? Well, your momma and me are going to be the man with the yellow hat and take you on a train and then stay in a hotel. Whew eee! We are gonna have some fun!"

Their smiles were infectious. Lisa's eyes were as big as saucers. She looked at me and pleaded, "Can we, Momma? Can we take an adventure with Lelia?" Jon is just learning to talk. But he evidently understood something great was about to happen. He squealed loudly and his short stubby legs tried to make him jump. Instead, he broke into a run into my arms.

"Yes, you can. We're all going. Except Daddy. He has to work. You can take one toy and one stuffed animal with you. I will pack everything else you need. Lelia is going to get her things packed. Everyone be ready in one hour!"

As we approached the automobile, the driver was loading our bags. With my baby on Lelia's hip and Lisa at my side holding my hand, I turned to my sweet husband and said, "Jon, thank you for helping me through this. I know this is only the beginning, but you helped me get off of my whiny bottom and get moving. I can't wait to get Ethel, Marie, and Suzy into a giant Nash sisters' hug. I don't know what to expect with Caroline. But I need to hug her neck too. We can get through this. We always do when we stick together."

~~~

Washington Union Station was mostly empty. It was weirdly quiet. I could smell the diesel engines idling in wait. As we approached the train tracks, I heard the station master calling, "All aboard track 3 for Richmond, Raleigh, and Atlanta. All aboard track 3." I turned to make sure we were all here together. Lelia was still carrying Jon Jr., and Lisa was clutching her hand as tight as she could. The heads of all three were swiveling to take in all the sights.

"Wowzah, Momma! It is big!" exclaimed Lisa.

Lelia was just as mesmerized, almost stumbling over Lisa. "Yes siree, Lisa, it sure is. Ain't it the biggest building you ever seen?"

I have to bring importance to every new adventure and said, "Yes, it is a big building. In fact, it might just be the biggest train station in the United States. And it's old. It was built around the time my Momma Flo was born. And that was a long time ago! We could take a train just about anywhere we want to from here."

Lelia's wide eyes caught mine, and she whispered, "But we are just gonna go to Raleigh, right?"

I nodded my head, leaned toward her and said, "Yes, today we are going to Raleigh, but who knows where we might go another day."

I turned around to make sure our suitcases were following us. The porter was bringing up the rear with six suitcases on a wagon. It looked like we were going for weeks with all those things. I really didn't know how long we would be gone. We would spend as much time in Raleigh as I needed to work things out with my sisters.

The porter helped us find our train car. "Ma'am, I'll take care of your luggage and help your girl find where she will be."

I stopped dead in my tracks. "What do you mean? My girl? Lelia is traveling with us."

The porter shifted his eyes from me to Lelia. Lelia looked at me and said, "Miss Walsh, I can't go with you. They have a special train car for people like me. I'll be fine. I ain't gonna get lost."

I put my hand on the wagon carrying the suitcases and held tight. "Sir, you don't understand. Lelia is with me. She is part of our family. I and the children need her with us. She will sit with us."

The porter was as gracious as he could be. "Suit yourself, but they will not let her sit up front with you. Whatever happens, I need to load the cases on another car. Please, ma'am."

"Okay. You go load our things," I said, placing several coins in his free hand. He pulled the wagon down the walkway toward the back of the train. I grabbed Lelia's arm and said emphatically, "You will sit with us."

Lelia's body was stiff, Lisa looked terrified, and Jon was crying in Lelia's arms. I led our group inside the train car, went toward the seat numbers that matched our tickets, and demanded that everyone sit down. No one objected. Our seats faced each other—two facing two.

I backed away and said to Lelia, "You sit by the window across from Lisa. My handbag and I will sit by the aisle."

Lelia evidently understood what I was doing and replied, "Thank you, Miss Walsh."

I have to admit I was anxious when the conductor came through. I noticed he was moving at a good clip through the train car, looking only at the aisle seats when he said, "Tickets please!"

I handed him all four tickets, he signed them, and looked at us. His eyes went from Lelia to me. "The Negro girl can't ride up here. Whites only."

This was one time I was happy that Jon was crying. He was bellowing, as if he understood the unfairness. Lelia was trying to settle him, but Jon would not have it. He reached a loud screeching yell. I leaned over to the conductor and shook my head and said, "Sir, I can't hear you. What are you saying?'

He leaned toward me to be heard over baby Jon, "I said Negros can't ride up with the whites. It is the law."

"Well, that is a problem, sir," I said loud enough for all to hear. "My baby will scream the whole way to Raleigh, North Carolina, if Lelia is not with him. And my son is not going to ride in another car without the family."

I looked around hoping for empathy from the other passengers. I caught the eye of a mother seated with an older child. She said to anyone who was listening. "Let them be. We don't want that baby crying for hours!"

Sitting a few seats behind us, another family was watching. There was a man wearing a military uniform, two children, and a baby in the woman's arms. The wife began to stand, but the husband put his hand on her shoulder. He stepped into the aisle, stood tall and straight, and approached the conductor, "I am Brigadier General James Baker, just returning home with my family. This is not a problem for anyone. Leave the family alone."

The conductor shook his head and moved toward

the officer. "I will lose my job over this, Brigadier General Baker."

The army officer faced the conductor moving with military stiffness. "Go get your boss. Tell him to come see me. I have fought many battles, and I can fight one more."

The conductor grunted and moved his way through the train car. I finally was able to exhale. There were such good people in this unfair world.

I looked over at Lelia. She had already begun to soothe Jon. As she hummed to my son, there were tears running down her cheeks. From this time on, I will never feel anything but compassion when hearing a crying baby.

It took longer than I expected it would to get to Raleigh on the train. I wish I would have driven us. When I'm driving, I am in control of speed, stops, and I can enjoy the views. Today, the train stopped too often, and I could rarely see anything interesting out our windows. Lisa, Lelia, and I were all miserable sitting so much. How many times can we walk the aisles on a train? I learned you can take at least 100 trips to see if other train cars have different views. Taking turns with Lisa, Lelia and I would challenge her to skip, jump an imaginary hopscotch, walk forward, backward, and sideways. And she got other children in the car to play Statues and Mother May I.

Jon was in hog heaven. He was in our arms for hours, eating, being sung to, or watching everything that was going on. Lelia snoozed for an hour or so while Jon slept on her chest.

I could not sleep. All I could do is worry about Caroline, the Parker children, this awful world where the government says people like Lelia are not as good as others so must be separated, and this war we are in that seems to never end. I couldn't wait to arrive in Raleigh and find my sister Ethel. Comfort would be in the refuge of the Nash sisters' hug.

CHAPTER 3

Marie

Gathering in a Palace

MOMMA TOLD ME TO TAKE the car and wait at the train station for Annie to arrive. Yippee! I love driving. Especially this car. A 1941 Pontiac Streamliner Torpedo. It is a blue beauty! It will be mine when I finish my first year of school at State College. Momma said it could motivate me to "pass my grade." I think it is just a way for her to show First-Dad-Frank that she is in control. I call him F-D-F when talking about him. But not to Momma. I call him Frank around Momma. His real name is Frank Pollard. He was Momma's first beau and is my legitimate father. Although the fact that he and Momma never got married made me illegitimate.

F-D-F decided I should have a car for college, so he just bought it. Momma was furious! She yelled and cussed for about an hour on the phone with him about buying me a car without her permission. It's not brand new. It's used. I didn't see the problem. But Momma and F-D-F have had their issues since I was born, so they rarely talk without fighting about something. Evidently, they finally agreed the car could be mine, but Momma was not going to let me have it until I finished my first year of college. She said she wanted to "break it in." I have no idea what she meant since someone had done that for four years before F-D-F bought it for me. After all, it's not a horse that needs to be broken. It's a car!

"Sure, Momma, I can go get Annie and the fam. You got any lettuce to fill up the tank?"

Momma looked at Now-Dad-Larry with an eye roll, then back at me with that momma sneer. "Don't talk like you're stupid. You don't need lettuce. You eat it. The fuel tank is full. Larry filled it just outside of Raleigh."

N-D-L stepped toward me, secretly slipped me a fiver, and said, "You'll be picking up Annie, Lelia, and the two children. Swing by the filling station and have them clean the windshield and interior. We want Annie, who has the greatest cars in the world, to be impressed with this one."

I grinned and blew him a kiss. N-D-L is a cool dad. Although I had some others that were pretty great too.

I eased the giant beauty out of the Hotel Sir Walter car park, and as soon as I was out of Momma's sight, I hit the gas pedal. Gliding through downtown Raleigh with the windows down and the radio playing was a gas. I couldn't wait to see Aunt Annie. I wish I could swing by and pick up Suzy, but there might not be enough room. I'll go get her later. Being together with the fam without my sister would be crazy.

Even though the train station was not far, I went out of my way to find a certain filling station. That boy I met at a dance last weekend said he worked at one on Hillsborough Street. Al, Alvin, Albert? I don't remember exactly. I do remember his red hair and that he was a jive cutter. The girls waited in line to cut a rug with him. I didn't have to. He came right up to me and said, "Come on, doll. Let's dance." And we did. For several songs.

Remembering that was like Whew! I think I need my oil checked.

I pulled into the Sunoco station. He said he worked there most afternoons. An older man came out toward the car wiping his hands with a rag. "Fill-er up?" he asked.

I felt a little foolish. Looked around a bit and replied, "Um . . . no, I was just wondering if you could check my oil, clean my windshield, or something."

The man walked to my window, bent down to look inside. He figured me out. "Okay. I can do that. But you don't need no fuel? Is there something else you really need? Maybe Al? Lotsa girls your age come round looking for Al."

I could feel my face heat up. How embarrassing. What was I thinking? He probably had a fistful of girlfriends.

The man put his hand on the car where the window was open. "Al's not here today. But I can tell him you came to call. What's your name?"

I quickly put the car in first gear, pushed in the clutch, and began to roll forward. "No. But thank you though," I said. He stepped away from the car, and I took off. How stupid am I?

~~~

I pulled into the pickup area of the train station, hoping to see them waiting so I wouldn't need to park. I'm a good driver, but I hate backing up to park. There were dozens of people waiting for a ride. None of them was my Aunt Annie. I could pick her out of a crowd, I thought. But not this crowd. I opened the door and stood on the side running board to see above the heads of people.

In the distance I heard someone singing/shouting. It was as familiar as my mother's voice when I was five years old.

"Ma rrie, Oh my little Ma rrie! You are the beauty of the fam i ly!"

I turned my head toward the sound. Not yet seeing her, I sang out, "Ann ee, NO, Ann ee, you are the beauty of the fam i ly!"

Then I spotted her. That beautiful, dark, wavy hair with just the perfect royal blue hat tilted to one side to make you notice her. She ran toward me. Her arms raised as if she was approaching the finish line of a race. A brown leather handbag was dangling from her arm. Very stylish, of course.

"Well, aren't you a sight for sore eyes, young lady!" she said, grabbing my arms and pulling me into a hug. There was that Nash auntie love! Uncontrollably, as we hugged, tears burst out of my eyes.

She pushed me back with both arms extended. "Let me take a look at my college-aged niece! I need to hear all about it!"

Before we could speak further, the rest of the Walsh family came up. Complete with Lelia. It was good to see them all. I had not seen baby Jon for a while. "Holy moly, JJ, look how you've grown! Are you reading yet? Riding a bike?" Everyone laughed.

Lisa jumped up toward my arms. "No, Marie, he is too little! That is me. I can read and ride a bike. Mommy, did we bring my bike?"

Annie was still staring at me. I wondered if she could tell how happy I was not only to see her but to tell her about my cool life.

Lelia spoke up, "Hey there, Miss Arie. You're pretty as a picture." I burst out laughing because I knew I was not. I was in my normal white blouse and black trousers. I had not even bothered to pull my hair back. Momma would have told me to find a bobby pin and get that hair out of your eyes!

I loved the way Lelia said my name. It sounded more like mis-ery than Miss Marie. I replied the same way I always did, "No, Lelia, today it's not so bad." I grabbed a bag from Lelia's hand and gave her a big smile.

After getting all the bags into the boot of the car, we got situated. Lelia and Lisa in the back. JJ and Annie up front with me.

Annie never missed a chance to talk about cars. "A mighty fine set of wheels here, little girl. Loving the color. Wowsa! You have a radio in here? Let's listen to that while you show me your driving skills. Have you named her yet?"

"Can't name her until I have made some memories

with her," I replied. "What are you driving now?"

"I don't drive much anymore. Jon has a driver assigned to him, so we can use him if we take any trips. I just take a taxi to go to the park with the children or the market for things. But if I needed a car, it would have to be American made. Jon is adamant about not riding in or driving a foreign car."

Then Annie leaned over and whispered, "But if I could buy the car of my dreams, it would be an Aston Martin. That is one sexy car!" She looked down at the seat between us, rubbed the leather seat and grinned like she was seeing Clark Gable sitting right beside us.

Perry Como's "Till the End of Time" came on the radio. "Oh, Aunt Annie, this song is a gas! He has the dreamiest voice!" I grabbed the volume knob and turned it way up.

From the backseat Lisa's excited voice said, "WHOA, Mommy, there's a radio in the car!"

"Yes siree, little girl. Your cousin Marie has a fine set of wheels!"

After I was sure we would not hear from Perry Como again, I turned down the volume and changed the subject. "Don't you just love this city? Momma said things have really changed since y'all started coming to see Caroline. When was the first time you came to Raleigh?"

"I believe the first time Caroline was taken to Dorothea Dix and we could see her was not long after you were born. I believe it was 1930 or 31. When we visited, we didn't see much of the town. I don't remember it really. All I knew was how small it was compared to

Washington. I had just moved up there."

As we turned down by the capitol building, Lisa spoke up. "Hey, Marie, are we gonna get some ice cream? It's hot in this town."

"I think I can find something like that. Y'all are staying in one of the finest hotels in the city. I am sure there will be ice cream. But I can't promise what flavor." That kid loved sweets like I do.

As we were getting closer to our destination, I said to them, "The Hotel Sir Walter is awaiting you!"

I looked back at Lelia and her eyes were as big as saucers. "Holy cow, look at that place. It looks fine! Are they gonna let me stay there?"

I hesitated and looked at Annie, then whispered, "I forgot to ask."

Annie was confident. "Lelia, we are going to work that out. We were successful on the train, and we will make it happen here too."

I had a solution. "Lelia, I have a big room at North Carolina State College. You can stay with me if they give you any flack. Then we can tell everyone Lelia is going to college! That'll be a hoot!"

"I can rest my head anywhere you tell me to." That giant smile of hers came out again. "But if we stay at college, I am gonna have to learn to drive. To get back and forth." We all laughed. Even JJ chuckled, and he had no idea what we were talking about.

Then Lisa chimed in. "Drive? Now that would be so funny! You are scared of riding a bike. You can't drive a car! Anyway, you have to stay with me, Lelia. I'll keep you safe."

Then Annie reminded me of the power of the Nash sisters. "Ethel will help me work this out. No one says no to Ethel. Together we are quite convincing. Don't you worry, Lelia."

Even though we were acting cool about this, I felt the anger rise up the back of my neck. I had heard all about the Jim Crow laws, but I never had to see them enforced. Of course, as a Negro woman, Lelia had to think about it all the time. This was going to be interesting.

There in the lobby of this lovely hotel sat Momma and N-D-L. Momma did not look happy. Oh geez. What has happened now. Annie dropped her bag and galloped across the lobby with Lisa holding one hand. Momma's face eased up and a smile crawled across it when Lisa ran and jumped in Momma's lap.

N-D-L walked over to Annie. He leaned in to give her a kiss on the cheek. "Hey, little Ann. Thank goodness you are here."

He looked at me, waved to Lelia, and quietly said, "I think you gals and I will sort out the suitcases and get you checked in. Lelia, can you get the children?"

Lelia's face now showed a bit of fear. "Yessir, Mr. Martin. But I don't want to cause no trouble."

N-D-L put his hand on her shoulder, "What kind of trouble are you fixin' to cause, Lelia?"

Lelia leaned toward him and whispered in his ear. "I'm a Negro."

He leaned back and with a loud guffaw said, "Naw, that can't be true! That ain't true!"

At first Lelia was taken aback. Then after a breath,

that smile glimmered. "Oh Mr. Martin, you know that can cause trouble in fancy places."

"Nope. Not here. Not when Larry Martin is around!"

Lelia moved JJ to the other hip and put her hand out for Lisa. With the two children attached to her, she walked tall right behind my sweet dad. I pulled up the rear with a very large dark-skinned bellman pulling the cart full of suitcases and bags. I wonder where they make him sleep.

~~~

Evidently N-D-L worked it all out at the front desk. We had no trouble as he led all of us but Momma and Annie to an elevator. We piled in. N-D-L pushed a button, and the doors closed. The loaded elevator began to move and did not stop for what seemed like a long time. When the elevator doors opened, we were facing right into the inside of a humongous house. My heart jumped. It seemed as if we had broken into someone's private space. N-D-L stepped forward like he was invited here. I took one step. Straight ahead I could see a huge living room through a tall archway. The room was full of furniture. Couches, tables, lamps, chairs. Well dang! It was just like a movie star's home I had seen in a *Look* magazine.

Taking another step and leaning forward, I noticed there were two hallways. I would say it looked like the dormitories at State College except the hall was as wide as a highway and there was carpet on the floor that spread almost to the edges and down to the end of the hall. On the left side I counted three closed doors on one side and a row of more windows than we had in our whole house on the other side. The light coming through the windows was so bright I knew we must be on the top floor. I headed down the other hallway. There were two closed doors then the carpet led you to turn right. So I did. I walked quietly so I wouldn't disturb anyone. Nearly a dozen closed doors lined this hallway. What the H?

Now it was me with an astonished smile. "Holy cow, this is amazing! How many rooms are in this place? Are you sure we're in the right place, Dad?"

"Yep, sure enough, Marie. Evidently Mr. Jonathan Vance Walsh is a big man in Raleigh. He arranged for us all to stay in this place. There are four bedrooms, six bathrooms, a kitchen, a playroom, living room, and a dining room. Ethel already decided who was sleeping where. So let's go. You youngsters aren't gonna believe this!"

He pointed down one hallway and described who was where. "Ethel and me are in this second room. That first door is one of the many bathrooms. There is another one on that side of the hall too. Nobody has to wait for a toilet here. The next door on this hall opens into our bedroom. They all look alike inside, so just remember your color. That room has blue everything. The walls, curtains, chairs, and bedspread are all some sort of blue. Ain't that something?"

I turned around to find the others. They were still in the elevator. Just stuck there. JJ was in Lelia's arms but not uttering a sound. Lisa's feet looked glued to the floor. I nervously giggled and said, "Come on, y'all.

You won't believe this!"

I took JJ from Lelia arms and said, "Come on. It's okay. Right, Dad? It's okay."

"Yes, dear girl, it's ours for a while." I twirled around and around, and JJ's feet sailed away from my hips. He began to laugh.

Lisa grabbed N-D-L's trousers and said, "It is so beautiful! Where do I go to sleep? I don't think I will be able to sleep!"

N-D-L grabbed Lisa's hand, motioned to Lelia and said, "Let's go see what else there is, ladies and gents."

We headed down the other hall. Pointing to the first door on the left, he said, "This room is for Annie and Daddy Warbucks, if he joins us. Lelia, there is a crib in there. Annie will have JJ with her. Notice Annie's room is the green room. Next to that is a sitting room/playroom. There is a door from the green room that opens directly into there. After the sitting room is a yellow room. That is yours, Lisa. Aunt Ethel says yellow matches your happy mood. So, she picked that one out for you. Of course, Lelia will stay with you. You each have your own bed in there. And a crib in case JJ wants to stay with his sister."

Lelia was walking around like someone drunk. She just kept looking all around, weaving, and stumbling into walls and doors. "I declare, Mr. Martin. This is the fanciest place I've ever seen. I cain't believe it. I just cain't believe I'm here! And nobody's gonna take me to jail for bein' in here."

To finish out the tour, N-D-L pointed back down toward the first hall. "Marie, there is one more bedroom. I think it is the gold room. That is for you and Suzy." I just stared into the room. It was stunning. The walls were papered with white and gold patterns. The curtains were a gold brocade. And there were two beds, each covered with the thickest quilts I'd ever seen. They were gold colored. I just stood there feeling like Lelia. How did we get so lucky?

N-D-L walked over to me, put his hand on my shoulder and said, "A little later you can go get Suzy to stay with you here. Ethel and Annie want their whole family around while we help Caroline." Then reality all came flooding back. Caroline, dear Caroline. The lump in my throat grew as large as my fist.

N-D-L turned quietly, gathered the rest of the group and said to me, "I'll give you a few minutes, sweet girl."

When he closed the door, I sank down on the bed wrapping the quilt around me to hold me tight. I cried like a baby. How dare I be so happy when Caroline is so sad, scared, and hurting? Oh Caroline, I am so, so sorry. My poor momma and Aunt Annie have a sister they don't seem to be able to help. I would die if Suzy and I couldn't help each other.

CHAPTER 4

Ethel

Getting Our Minds Right

ANNIE AND I TALKED FOR nearly an hour in the lobby of the Hotel Sir Walter. I started out telling her how angry I was about men flapping money around.

"Do you see this place, Annie? It's grossly expensive! It's showboating for Jon to put us up here. We don't have this kind of money, and I don't want to be with this kind of folk!"

Annie took a look around at the furniture in the lobby. "It is lovely, isn't it? The furniture is exquisite. Why don't we deserve to stay in a place like this if Jon can afford it? Maybe the owner of the hotel put all the money in the lobby and the rooms are just normal."

"Naw, they aren't! Larry and I went upstairs to the rooms that Jon arranged for us. There was enough dough spent on those rooms to feed all the farmers in North Carolina! Why didn't Jon just get us a regular place? We don't need a luxury vacation when our sister is in the asylum!"

With gigantic bad timing, a young woman in a tight black dress and a pressed white apron came by with a tray of crystal glasses full of champagne. I almost blew my top!

Annie's smart enough to see when my top might come off. With a small wave of her hand, she sent the girl away. She was used to dismissing the help.

I leaned in to spout off more anger. She put her finger up to her lips and firmly said, "Shut up, Ethel. You're being ridiculous. Jon did this for me. He knew how upset I was about Caroline and not hearing from you. I was distraught. He wanted to help us. He wanted to make this easier. And by the way, it's the closest hotel to Dix Hill."

By this time, I saw the veins in Annie's forehead building up. It looked like they were going to explode. I've seen that before. I moved to the back of the sofa to take a breath. A Nash woman exploding is not pretty. Especially in public.

"Okay, calm down. We can work this out later," I said to keep the explosion from happening.

Annie fell back into the sofa and declared, "We will not argue anymore. You'll just say thank you to Jon. And to me."

I wish I'd taken the champagne because our discussion wouldn't get better. I had to tell her about Caroline and schizophrenia. I told her about talking again to Nurse Joanna. I shared as much as I could without the whole world of Hotel Sir Walter knowing our business. I knew we couldn't go upstairs and share all this in front of the girls.

I brought my back up straight on the sofa, crossed my legs at the ankles and pushed my feet firmly on the floor. My hands were in my lap clasped together. Annie scooted closer to me.

"They have a word for Caroline's brain disease—schizophrenia. It means a split mind. People like Caroline cannot understand what's real and what's not. She sees things and hears things that no one else does. In this case, Caroline was sure she was being bombed by the Japanese, and she could hear it all. To her, the Parker children were in danger, and it was her job to keep them safe. So, she took them to the basement of the house and locked the door. Before she lost all reality, she called me. By the time the medics arrived at the house, she had tied the children to chairs so they could not escape. According to what Caroline told the doctors, they kept screaming. To keep the Japanese from hearing them, Caroline told us later she began to stuff rags in their mouths when she heard noises upstairs."

Annie had been holding her breath apparently because it all whooshed out when she said, "Oh God, Ethel! How does that happen? Caroline loves those children!"

"That's the craziness. Joanna told me that the need to protect is strong even when the threat is not real. If Caroline didn't care for them so much, she would have just run away. But here's the thing, Annie. The police do not care how much she likes them. She was abusing them. When she's stable, they'll charge her."

Annie's head fell into my lap. She began sobbing.

I stroked her back and whispered to her, "I know. I know. It's terrible. I don't know what to do."

The woman with the champagne came back around and asked if we needed anything. I sat up straighter and wiped my face with my handkerchief. I always carry one in my dress pocket. "I think we'll have that champagne now," I said graciously.

I tossed down that sweet liquid. Annie held off on the liquid motivator and began to compose herself. It took her a minute, but she worked up the nerve to ask, "How is Caroline? What did they do to her?"

"As I told you on the phone, they have her heavily medicated. I haven't seen her. You and I have an appointment tomorrow at nine with Dr. Redmond. Joanna and Belle will be there. Joanna said they will talk more about therapies and medication."

"Ethel, how can they charge her with anything if she is so sick?"

Tears swelled up in my eyes. "I don't know. I don't feel like I know anything. Sister, I'm glad you are here. We don't have Momma or Dianne anymore. We just have each other to slog through this."

"Yes, Ethel. We can figure it out by working together."

When we got up from the sofa, Annie linked her arm through mine. "Come on, Ethel. Let's go look at these luxury suites. We can act like we are rich enough to conquer the world."

Of course, she could make me smile through tears.

The rest of the day was spent with family. Marie had picked up Suzy from the guest house at Dix Hill.

She was as impressed as the rest of us. We all gathered around the elegant dining table with plenty of tea, coffee, Coca Cola, and water—whatever we wanted. We stayed away from the subject of Caroline and acted as if everything was okay. But we knew it certainly was not. As Momma used to say to us and as I often said to Marie and Suzy, "We are not the most pitiful here."

I tried to get everyone to think of the good in the world. We could not come up with much good in 1945. Happiness is sometimes hard to find.

Larry found the first good thing, "Baseball!" he said. "The All-American Girls League is keeping us interested, and the Major League is still hanging in. I just listened to the Senators beat the pants off Detroit. And those Tigers have been beating everyone."

Since I was leading the discussion, I said, "I figure that's a good thing. But you are the only one who cares about baseball."

Marie piped in, "I love baseball! Boys are always talking about it. Suzy and I have to stay up on it."

Suzy added, "And don't forget how good the women are at this sport. We ought to be proud of the females!"

Then my sister thinks of a good thing for her. "I am most grateful for an end to the war in Europe. Even though Jon did not have to be over there, his job at the Pentagon working for General Somervell is like he was away. That War Department might as well be in Europe as Washington, DC. He is never home, but now maybe he will be."

Suzy was not going to let it go at that. "Oh yeah,

Aunt Annie, but don't forget that many men and women won't be coming back to their families. I heard on the radio that nearly 400,000 United States men and women have been killed. And they haven't stopped counting. We are still in a war outside of Europe. And Japan . . ."

I stopped her in her tracks. We had to come back to good things. "Suzy, we're trying to find good in this world to take our mind off our own problems. Stay focused, girlie."

With her voice louder than it should be with her mother, Suzy countered "But, Momma, you can't ignore the horror in this world!"

The room was silent. She was right. I hate when that happens.

There was a knock at the door and a man announced room service. Marie went to the door and led him to the living area where we were now all gathered. When I saw the cart, I knew I had to stop this foolishness. "We have already eaten. We didn't ask for that. How much will it cost?"

Marie cut in, which was not smart. "I ordered it, Mother dear. Lisa and I decided we needed ice cream in this perfect palace. Besides, they told me dessert is free. You just need to give him a tip."

Annie said, "Ethel, calm down. I got this. We did indeed promise Lisa that we would have ice cream."

The man who wheeled the cart into the room just stood there looking from me to Marie to Annie. "It is okay, ma'am. No tip needed." He turned quickly and almost ran to the elevator jumping in as soon as the doors opened.

I started to laugh. Then Larry joined in with his distinctive guffaw. "Ethel, you scared that man nearly to death!" We all started laughing and could not stop. The whole room seemed to be shaking like a cheap dance floor. Lelia rushed into the room with both children saying, "What's so funny? We want in!"

"Ice cream, Lelia!" In her singsong voice, Marie declared, "I scream, you scream, we all scream for ice cream!"

Suzy and Marie served us. There were three flavors of ice cream—vanilla, strawberry, and chocolate. My family always dives into the chocolate first. While waiting for our serving, no one talked. It was like a litter of pigs waiting for their momma to lie down already. Once served, spoons hitting bowls of sweetness, slurping mouths, and groans of happiness were the only noises in this elegant room. At that point, our time together was a lot like many family moments of happiness and love.

Annie put her bowl down and went to gather her son from Lelia. That little sugar easily snuggled on her chest. As Annie began to leave the room, she came over to me, shifted Jon, and put her skinny arms around my thick body squeezing hard. Whispering in my ear she said, "Dianne and Momma are here with us. They are going to help us help Caroline." Even though I wasn't done being mad about all the money being thrown around, I hugged her back.

As we unlocked from the Nash sisters hug, she planted a kiss on my cheek. Turning to the others in the room she said, "Goodnight, my beloved family.

The greatest good things in my life right now are the people in this room and all the Nash goodness that came before us. Everyone, sleep tight."

Lisa was dreamily leaning against Lelia. Her belly full of sugar. "Sleep tight, beloved Mommy."

CHAPTER 5

Annie
A Mind of Her Own

I WAS IN THE KITCHEN bright and early. Larry was there unpacking breakfast sandwiches, coffee, orange juice, and milk from brown paper bags. "I found this great diner just down the street," he said. "The smell took me there—bacon, coffee, and cigarettes." Swinging his hand across the counter full of food he commented, "All this for half the price of just coffee ordered in here. How are you feeling this morning, Annie?"

"I am starved! Thank you, Larry. I slept pretty well considering what needs to happen today. JJ was in my bed breathing heavily right beside me. The breathing of a sleeping child is so calming. Anybody can sleep to that music."

Larry made a grunting noise and smiled wide. "Yeah, that's what Ethel says about my sleep breathing." With impeccable timing as always, Ethel entered the room. "Sleep breathing? More like a lumberman's saw cutting down a hundred-year-old tree." She patted his protruding belly as she walked by.

I sat with my coffee at the table, added two teaspoons of sugar and a good-sized dollop of cream. I started to bite into the egg and bacon sandwich. Ethel stared with amazement. "SISTER, how do you keep your girlish figure when you eat like that?"

Just to show off I said, "My mind runs a mile a minute all day long. Food doesn't have a chance to fatten me up. Besides, I have Daddy's body shape. You and Dianne got Momma's."

Ethel did not see the humor in that. She looked at Larry hoping for a comeback. But he just raised his arms with his palms up. "Leave me out of this." Then grabbing his breakfast and coffee, he escaped to the living room.

Ethel and I spent the next half hour going over the plans for our day. We decided last night who would lead the conversations with Dr. Redmond, Nurse Joanna, and Belle. Belle was going to be the most difficult. She is such a dear, dear person. But she is bound to be furious at Caroline for hurting her grandchildren. Ethel reminded me that Belle must be angry at herself for setting up Caroline to move in with her son's family—to have trusted Caroline. I am still very nervous about how to talk with a group of people with all these emotions stirring around the room like thick smoke from a wet fire.

And all this has to be resolved before being able to see Caroline. Ethel is usually tough as nails, but this morning she said, "I'm afraid I will be a blubbering idiot with Caroline and not be able to speak a word. I am sad. It is all just sad."

I quit twirling a lock of my hair and reached over to Ethel. "It is the saddest thing in the world. But I'm angry. They should have known! They are medical professionals after all! She has only been living outside of Dix Hill for three months. That was too soon for her to be on her own. How did they not know?"

Ethel stood up, breathed deeply and repeated words I had heard us say to each other most of my life. "We don't have time for sadness, we have got to pull together. We Nash sisters always stick together."

Just then, Marie and Suzy entered the kitchen. Without hesitation, Marie said, "I'm ready to go with you. Suzy and I decided last night that I should go and she would stay to prepare what was needed from here."

Ethel was adamant, as she usually is. "No, you can't go. You don't need to be involved in all this."

Marie calmly stepped closer to her mother. "I just heard you say that Nash sisters always stick together. How about the Nash women? Suzy and I are part of this family. I am now 18 and you have sent me away to college. Don't you think it's time I really understand our family? Isn't it time for me to pitch in as an adult?"

I knew how they felt. As a younger sister, I often felt left out when we were in our early years. Moving to Marie and Suzy, I put my hands on their shoulders. "Yes, you are both becoming young women. But today is not the day to be indoctrinated into adulthood. Ethel and I will go alone. Then we can sort out all of this with the two of you, Larry, and Jon. I love you for wanting to help. That is a sure sign of a Nash family member. Ethel and I are not even sure what we are walking into today. Tonight, when we return, we will all talk about the best way to help Caroline. A good plan can be built when we know the reality."

Ethel took her two daughters in one big hug. "Doggonit, girls, how did you become so wonderful with a momma like me."

Larry stepped into the room. "Ladies, your taxi awaits downstairs. Marie, I think I need a tour of State College today. You, me, and Suzy will see the whole place. I hear they're building a thousand-ton granite monument settin' on over 500 tons of concrete over there. I want to see that."

I went back to the children's rooms. When I walked into the room, Lelia was up, dressed, and beginning to get the children ready for the day. I told her our plans and asked her to keep my children close. She held her eyes on mine and said, "Miss Walsh, you try to find happiness in this day. We will be here when you come back. I know Jesus will be with you."

Turning around, the tears began to flow. Right then I could see no happiness in the day we were beginning.

~~~

The taxi driver approached the all-too-familiar campus of Dorothea Dix State Hospital. We have been visiting for nearly 15 years. Once through the main gate, I gave him the directions to get to the hospital. He evidently had not been there before. Lucky man.

We drove past the enormous oak trees, homes for staff, the larger residential homes for patients, the gardens, and baseball fields. As we drew near the looming hospital for the insane, it was deceiving.

Most people driving by would have no idea who is in there and what they needed. The tall sturdy iron fence enclosed a grand four-story building. There was grass dotted with flower beds. Picnic tables were shaded under large oak trees. It looked like a city park in Washington, DC. But I knew it was a prison for the criminally insane. My heart began to race, I reached for Ethel's hand. She grasped mine lovingly. Wanting to provide some comfort for both of us, I whispered, "Lelia said Jesus is with us."

Ethel responded, "I don't think Jesus is anywhere near us today. He needs to be in Japan. We are on our own."

As we enter the hospital, I am flooded with memories of visiting Caroline here the first time. I don't think I feel any more mature or less scared than that day. The lobby felt just as vast and the situation no less terrifying. But back then I had two sisters with me. Now it is only Ethel and me.

Because Ethel was the oldest and more experienced with this place, we decided she would be in charge first. I walked a few steps behind her, not to acquiesce but to hide from this situation. We went to the desk, told the receptionist who we were, and said we were here to see Dr. Redmond about our sister Caroline Nash. She nodded, plugged in the telephone cord to a switchboard and said, "Caroline Nash's family is here."

Goodness gracious. They had all been talking about us. They knew us by just that statement, Caroline Nash's family is here.

Ethel stepped back from the desk, looked at me and spoke firmly, "Breathe, Annie, breathe deeply. We have the guts to do this. Let's show them that. Stand up straight."

Unlike our previous visits, the doctor came down the stairway to us. He reached out and shook first Ethel's hand, then mine. He took a step closer to be discreet. "Caroline is sleeping well. This will give us plenty of time. I have reserved a room for us to talk. Nurse Dunn and Mrs. Parker are available to meet with us, but I thought I would ask how you would like to proceed. Shall we ask them to join us now or after I answer any questions you may have?"

I looked at Ethel and nodded my head. My hand went to my hair and began lacing the locks of hair around my fingers. Over and over again. I hadn't said the words out loud, but I wasn't quite ready to hear the truth. Ethel knew the details of the episode from Nurse Joanna days ago, but I wasn't sure I wanted to hear it all right now. And I was sure I could not face Belle Parker yet.

Ethel read my mind, looked at me and then the doctor. "Doctor, we need to get this information in pieces. We are not as tough as we look. Can we talk to you first?"

Geez, I love my sister.

"Very well, Mrs. Martin. Let's do that. Mrs. Walsh, does that meet your needs also?"

"Of course," I said. The twirling of my hair subsided.

We entered a room with a large table and ten chairs. There was a blackboard with medical terms written on it. I could not look away. The words appeared with large circles drawn around groups of words as if to rope them into control and some big words at the top. To me they were jumbled and not understandable. I saw scary words like ADDICTION, SCHIZOPHRENIA, PSYCHOSIS, BRAIN INJURY on the board.

I froze in front of the chalkboard, scrutinizing the lassoed words. The room smelled of chalk. The words were smears of chalk.

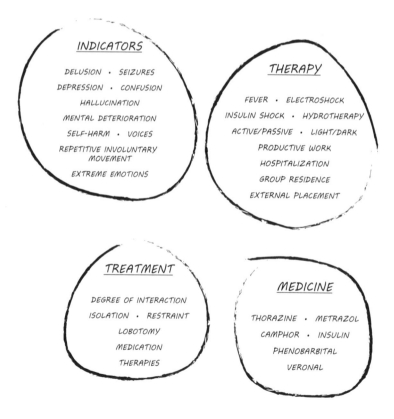

INDICATORS

DELUSION · SEIZURES
DEPRESSION · CONFUSION
HALLUCINATION
MENTAL DETERIORATION
SELF-HARM · VOICES
REPETITIVE INVOLUNTARY MOVEMENT
EXTREME EMOTIONS

THERAPY

FEVER · ELECTROSHOCK
INSULIN SHOCK · HYDROTHERAPY
ACTIVE/PASSIVE · LIGHT/DARK
PRODUCTIVE WORK
HOSPITALIZATION
GROUP RESIDENCE
EXTERNAL PLACEMENT

TREATMENT

DEGREE OF INTERACTION
ISOLATION · RESTRAINT
LOBOTOMY
MEDICATION
THERAPIES

MEDICINE

THORAZINE · METRAZOL
CAMPHOR · INSULIN
PHENOBARBITAL
VERONAL

Dr. Redmond walked to the chalkboard and pulled a wooden panel to cover the board, hiding the words. However, they were seared on my brain. Ethel reached to gently pull my arm toward a chair that faced away from the chalkboard.

"Dr. Redmond, can we have some water?"

I could hear a crackle in her voice. She was also disturbed by what we saw.

"Of course," he said as he walked to a cabinet at the end of the room and picked up a telephone. "Please bring a pitcher of cold water for two and a pot of tea. We are in room five."

Ethel held on to my arm and gave me a small squeeze. Her eyes made direct contact with mine. It felt like she was sending me mental messages. I nodded my head, giving permission for us to move on.

Dr. Redmond sat across the table from us, placing a thick file in front of him. The label on the substantial file said NASH, CAROLINE. There was my sister. Bound up in years of papers.

"Mrs. Martin, Mrs. Walsh, I know this must be distressing for you. I hope you trust that we at Dorothea Dix care about Caroline's well-being. I would like to tell you a little about her mental and medical condition at this time. Then I can answer any questions that you have about the treatment and prognosis for Caroline."

My mind flashed back to those words on the chalkboard.

Ethel nodded her head. "Dr. Redmond, I need to ask you something before we go ahead. What is the bottom line? Is Caroline going to be okay?"

There was a knock at the door. A woman in a starched gray dress cinched at the waist with a black belt entered. She wore white socks and shoes. She was carrying a tray of water, tea, and some cookies that looked like Snickerdoodles. Caroline's favorite. I lowered my head and began to weep. Ethel, who notices everything, said in a sing-song voice, "Snickerdoodles—America's Favorite Cookie!" We heard that line on the radio recently.

The woman smiled at both of us and left the room. She looked familiar. I will ask Ethel later about that.

Dr. Redmond poured the water into two glasses and poured hot tea in a cup for himself.

"Mrs. Martin, you are right. That is the most important question. At this point I cannot say with certainty. What I do know is that we have been treating Caroline much of her life, and we know she has amazing resilience. Although the latest circumstance seems dire, I feel with time and treatment she will recover. How much and how fast, I don't know. In my experience people like Caroline draw tremendous strength from their family. With your help and many visits, I believe she will be able to pull on that strength to will herself well."

Ethel spoke as if she was preaching the Lord's words, "Dr. Redmond, Caroline is a Nash sister. We will be by her side until we die."

For the next hour Dr. Redmond talked about mental illness in general and Caroline's specific case. He used many of the words written on the chalkboard and by bringing them into context, the fear of those words began to melt away.

"Caroline had a psychotic episode. She was experiencing delusions based on unfounded fears. There were noises which she believed were bombs. When she felt they were close and she and the children were in danger, her protective instincts took over. We all believe that Caroline meant no harm to the children. I have interviewed Caroline. She has been unable to explain all that was happening. This is not unusual. Often people experiencing extreme trauma will not be able to remember. Mrs. Martin, the details you provided from the frantic phone call from Caroline gave us information to help diagnose and recommend treatment.

"When Caroline was admitted to the hospital, she was combative, screaming, and unable to calm herself or control her body movements. We needed to restrain her until the medication began to sedate her. It was most important that she not harm herself or others. Nurse Dunn let me know that you talked to Caroline once more before the medication took full effect. For the past 24 hours, we have kept her calm with medication so her brain and body can rest. We have slowly reduced the dosage so that in the last hour she has been awake. She is still very tired and sleepy, but she is past this episode. Now we need to work on a long-term plan for her wellness. I know this is a lot to take in. Do you have questions?"

I felt a bit medicated too. I was impressed that I could be still and listen to Dr. Redmond and not react. It was as if he was talking about someone other than my sister. I looked over at Ethel. She was looking at her hands clasped in her lap. Her hands were moving in a rhythmical manner like snakes crawling over and around each other again and again.

I spoke next. "Dr. Redmond, I have so many questions. I don't know where to begin. Can you give my sister and me a few minutes, then bring in Nurse Joanna Dunn and Mrs. Belle Parker? Maybe if we have the full picture from their perspectives, it will answer some questions before they are asked."

"Yes, of course," the doctor responded. "Would you like something more to drink or eat?"

Ethel finally stopped rubbing her hands and spoke up, "I would like a drink of whiskey if that is anywhere near." At first, I thought she was kidding, but she was not.

Dr. Redmond did not seem surprised by this request. He evidently has this kind of discussion all the time, and he knew how people reacted. "Mrs. Martin, I am afraid alcohol is not allowed anywhere on the grounds." With a barely detectable smile, he whispered, "But I happen to know Raleigh is full of places where you can enjoy a moderate amount of that kind of medicine."

It was a nice break of tension. As he left the room, we both began a quiet giggle. For me it was to cover up the anxiety. I leaned over to Ethel and said, "You were about to rub your hands raw. I was worried I would have to pick up a few fingers off the floor."

She quickly responded, "Turn around and let me look at the back of your head. Have you twisted your hair right out of your scalp?" Although I knew I had been still as a statue, I put my hand back there to feel for a bald spot, just in case.

Ethel and I discussed what we heard. And what might happen next for Caroline. The episode must have been horrifying for Caroline and the children. The trip to Dix Hill and the restraint also sounded terrifying. We both agreed that for now, Caroline could not be in a better place. The doctor and medical staff knew her so well, and they cared for her. Even though I wanted to grab her up and take her home to get well, I realized that was not possible. Ethel reminded me, "Where is home, Annie? We don't have a home with Dianne, Momma, and Caroline's bedrooms anymore. Right now, Caroline must stay here."

There was a knock on the door. We pulled ourselves together and reached for more water and the cookies that had been brought to us. We needed something to get us through the next hour or so. Maybe Snicker-doodles would help.

"Come in," I said.

As the door opened, we both stood. First Dr. Redmond entered, then Nurse Joanna. There was a pause in the entourage. It seemed as if no one else was coming. Then Belle Parker slowly walked through the door. It felt like lawyers and witnesses entering a courtroom. And Belle Parker was the victim. My throat was closing. Tears filled my eyes and fell down my cheeks as Belle came to us and gave us a warm hug. Then something happened I never dreamed would. Ethel fell into Belle's arms, pushing her head onto Belle's chest and sobbed. She was crying so hard that her words were muddled. Ethel just kept saying over and over again, "I am sorry. I am sorry. I am so sorry."

I was witnessing my older sister regress to childhood being held by Momma. Belle held the hug as Ethel began to relax and become quiet. Those two women were bound as if they were grieving as one. Then Belle extended her arms to look into Ethel's face. She held her gaze, then looked over at me—inviting me into this moment.

"I know," Belle said ever so softly. "I'm sorry too." Although their skin color was different and their life experience had been so separate, right then they were kin. They were sisters in sorrow.

Finally, we composed ourselves and sat at the table. Dr. Redmond gave a brief summary of what we already talked about. Maybe for Joanna's sake, but I really appreciated it too.

"Nurse Dunn, you only came to know Caroline a few months ago. Let me give you a little context. Caroline came to us at the age of 15. There was a fire in a barn at her home. She was burned over much of her body and had several life-threatening injuries. The medical hospital took care of the physical wounds, then Caroline came here to work on her mental wounds. She has been a model for people with mental illness. She has cooperated with all the treatment and therapies here. She became a fine citizen at Dorothea Dix. We have all benefited from her hard work, her love and care for the children, and her contributions to each group home where she has lived. We have some of the most prolific gardens in North Carolina because of Caroline. She also took great care of the animals on our campus. I believe you arrived just as her treatment was elevated to living off the campus."

He continued, but this time was speaking to Belle. "Mrs. Parker, what I just witnessed was the most generous and compassionate moment I have ever known. Thank you."

Belle stood as she spoke. "I have been with Caroline for nearly 15 years. I have watched her grow, change, and become a fine person in every way. She has a loving, supportive family, but I feel like she is family to me also. Even though she terrified my grandchildren, I know she did it out of love. She is not well; my heart and head know she was protecting my babies as any mother would. I meant what I said. I am sorry this happened to the children and most importantly to Caroline. My grandchildren will be okay. They are confused, but they are already asking where Caroline is. Caroline is the damaged one. Something happened that she could not control."

I stood and officially pronounced, "You, Belle Parker, are family! You have been since we met you. No offense to you, Dr. Redmond, but no amount of medicine or treatment for Caroline could have worked for Caroline the way that you, Belle, have helped her. You have been by my sister's side every day through her fears, anxiety, and while she was learning to be a good person despite her disabilities. For all of the Nash sisters and the generations to come, we owe you."

Ethel piped in, "Yeah we do. BIG TIME!"

For the next few hours, we learned more about the medication and Caroline's recovery thus far. Nurse Joanna is perfectly equipped with knowledge, experience, and kindness that will be able to help Caroline. I am convinced of that.

Belle talked about her role in the future. "We have all decided that I will stay on as Caroline's caregiver. I will help get her reoriented to the people and this place. But we will not know for a week or so how to proceed. We are letting Caroline show us what she can handle and when.

To conclude the discussion, Dr. Redmond gave us the bad and good news. He told us we would not be able to see Caroline today. He said we had to wait until she was stable and the anxiety had subsided. He added that most likely they would wait for Caroline to ask to see us. He also reassured us when he said, "Caroline has been accepting of and responsive to treatment in the past. She can do that again."

I needed to have this meeting conclude, so I thanked them all and stood. "Dr. Redmond, Nurse Dunn, and Belle, I feel so much better now. It sounds like this will be another long road. With the benefit of your intelligence and caring, we will be able to stand strong for Caroline. We can stay as long as we need to. Our families know this takes priority over everything. We will be back every day."

In the end, I was feeling a fraction of happiness to such a sad day. I grabbed Ethel's hand under the table. It was warm and so familiar. It felt the same as Momma's soft, wrinkly hand. Momma is watching over us. I am sure of it.

We stood to leave the room. "You know what, Dr. Redmond?" I asked. Ethel was reading my mind. She joined me in finishing that phrase that has always been true, "The Nash sisters are going to be just fine."

We left the room and walked down the hallway arm in arm. I was exhausted. It felt as if we had just fought in a battle and were pulling each other out of the trenches. We entered the lobby where we began this long, long day. There sat Jane Hines in one of the upholstered chairs that were in a row against the wall. She was flipping through files of papers. I could tell she was not really concentrating. She was just shuffling them. I picked up our pace and called her name. "Jane? Jane Hines!"

Jane stood abruptly and the papers scattered all over the floor. Standing very still, she eyed us as if she was a deer in the yard trying to assess the danger in moving forward.

Ethel, with a gust of energy nearly shouted to Jane saying, "Oh, girl! You are a friendly sight for sore eyes!"

Jane came forward and thrust out her hand. Ethel reminded her who we were, "Don't stick your hand out like we don't know each other! Come on in for a hug. I need a hug from someone with no bad news!" We all laughed and came in for that hug.

The tension eased, but Jane was still careful. "It's so good to see you. I'm sorry we are seeing each other under these circumstances. How are you?"

I replied honestly. "We are dog-tired and drained.

Let's go outside and visit under one of those giant oak trees."

Jane gathered her papers in no particular order and stuffed them back in the files. I knew she hated disorganization, but she was sacrificing for us.

Outside it was warm. Ethel had something to say about it, as usual. "Jumpin' Jehoshaphat! It is hot as hades out here."

I had almost forgotten it was summer. It seemed like we were in that room for weeks. When we reached the shade, the temperature dropped at least ten degrees.

"Whew, that's better," said Ethel.

We sat down at one of the wooden picnic tables. I knew it, as all the others, had been made by patients. And most likely had been sanded and kept splinter free by someone like Caroline over the years.

"Ethel, Annie, I was able to investigate what happened with Caroline. As you probably know, she is experiencing some really challenging developments. I asked Dr. Redmond to permit me to attend the planning meetings for her so I can stay really close to her progress. Dr. Redmond is allowing that. How are you feeling about what you learned with Dr. Redmond's team today?"

I was back to my state of organizing next steps. "Jane, I don't really know what I feel. We learned a lot, and I need time to process it all. I wish I had taken notes, but there was no way I could do that. When I have settled, I will write down what I can remember. Maybe Ethel and I can recreate the important points together. It would be helpful if, when we get a first draft, you could read it and fill in the blanks."

"Of course, I am happy to help."

Wiping her brow with the handkerchief from the pocket of her dress, Ethel asked a most important question. "Jane, I think I heard time and time again that Caroline is worse than she has ever been but that Dr. Redmond thinks she can beat this. You are a smart woman. You train all the nurses. And you know us pretty well. What do you think?"

With an official pause I have seen Jane do in the past, she moved into clinical mode. "Caroline has moved into full schizophrenia. If you want to understand that better, I can bring you some text books and research papers to read. I believe she has been progressing in that direction for years—maybe all her life. But she had been able to overcome or cope with those symptoms. As sometimes happens, her brain 'snapped.' It could no longer be controlled by her coping mechanisms or medication. It will take a while to find out why. But the answer to that question may help with effective treatment."

My muscles were turning weak. I wasn't sure I could hold myself up much longer. Jane's information did not surprise me or even terrify me. I just felt anesthetized. I leaned my head on Ethel's shoulder.

Ethel spoke for us. "Jane, I think we need to get back to the hotel. This is all too much. I feel like I could sleep for a week. Thanks for helping. We will need your help for a long time. We need information, the truth, and all the care we can get. But right now, I need a drink. Then a bed."

"I understand. I thank you for letting me help. In times of trouble, friends never know what to do. To start with, I can drive you back to the hotel."

Chapter 6 — December 1945

Nash Round-Robin Letters

December 15, 1945

Momma, Aunt Caroline, Aunt Annie, Suzy, and all the men associated with our Nash family,

Thanks, Momma, for letting me start the Nash Round-Robin Letters. It is super swell that we have the family history in this way. During our visit to Momma and Larry's this weekend, Suzy and I re-read the old letters. I asked Momma if she thought everyone had time to start them up again. She thought it might just be the tonic we all need.

And this will give me a chance to practice my handwriting. They really make a fuss about legible handwriting here at State College.

The last letter in Momma's box was dated 1943. The US was knee deep in war with no end in sight. It only became our war when Japan attacked Pearl Harbor. But we couldn't seem to accomplish much except letting our troops be killed by the thousands. It was a depressing time. Maybe that is why you stopped writing to each other.

School is out for the holidays. I have finished my exams and think I did okay. I was taking five classes this semester and that is way too many at once. My home room professor advised me to take a heavy load to show everyone women could handle anything. I have become a flag she likes to wave. I heard her tell another professor, "Marie is just what we need to push our woman engineer numbers over 50. She is smart, the first woman from the family to attend college, and she's a North Carolinian." When I told Momma about that, her remark was pretty much what we all would expect, "That and 20 cents can buy you a cup of coffee."

Anyway, Momma. I hear your voice every time I do well on a test or get something right when I have to raise my hand to show what I know. I say to myself, "Well, there is another 20 cents when I graduate."

I am home for Christmas and helping Momma with the laundry part of the business. She shut down the ice cream business for this year. She says, 'If it doesn't bring in the bread, we can't keep doing it."

N-D-L—You all know that is what I call Larry. I have three dads so far. This is my way to keep them apart in my mind. Sorry, Larry, if you are reading this. But it's better than calling you dad # 3. Anyway, he decided to try out a new job. He is driving long haul trucks, delivering stuff to stores all over the South. Right now, he is gone for three weeks. It is good that Suzy and I are around to help with the business. Suzy likes the washing part. I like the folding part. There is a particular way shirts and pants should be folded. I like doing it with clean edges. If I fold just right, there is less ironing needed. I hate the ironing part. As you all know, if you don't do the ironing just right, Momma will throw it back in the basket, and that means I have to start over. I hear Grandma Flo taught the Nash girls that.

School is really fun. I have met tons of new people. The school tells you everything you are supposed to do, so if you follow the rules you don't get in trouble. I don't like the woman that manages the house where six of us live. She is called a housemother, but I don't think she ever had children. She thinks everyone is up to no good. Sally, one of the girls in the house, likes to play more than she likes to go to class. It was the last straw just before exams when the housemother caught her kissing a boy on the porch of the house. And we also heard the porch light was on. At breakfast the next morning, the housemother said her behavior would bring a bad reputation to the house. Then Sally was told she had to "leave this respectable home." That is when I learned how important it is to kiss out back with the lights out. (Just kidding, Momma.)

Annie, the home where we live reminds me of the place you lived when you first moved to DC. I thought that was a most marvelous place for girls to live together. I will always remember us visiting you when you were so sick those many years ago. You didn't even have a house-mother, did you? And you weren't much older than I am now. This house has five bedrooms for two girls to a bedroom, the housemother's room and a guest room. It has a big dining room and parlor. We do most of our studying in the parlor.

My roommate is Isabelle Arrington. We call her Izzy. We get along well. She grew up in Durham. Her dad is a big man at the tobacco company there. Izzy will flat out tell you the best part of that is getting free cigarettes. Her dad wants her to hand them out at State College so his sales will rise. And no, Momma, I do not smoke. I don't like the taste or the smell. And I am scared to death of a fire. The girls can't smoke in the house, thank God, so all the smoking happens in the yard or walking around campus.

Speaking of Durham, baseball is back! The local team used to be called the Durham Tobac-conists, but there hadn't been a baseball team in town for a while. Now a team is back, and they are called the Durham Bulls. I can't wait to go see them! N-D-L, please come with me in the spring!

I'll stop for now and let you all tell your stories. When I am back at school, I can mail a letter from State College pretty cheap so I don't have to cut into my 20 cents for coffee.

I love you all!

Marie

December 21, 1945

Hello sweet family!

When Ethel told me that we were going to start up the Nash Round-Robin Letters again, I realized I did not have a typewriter. Since I no longer work at the War Department, I don't have a way to write a letter. Yes, I know I could write longhand, but anyone that has seen me write even a recipe knows my handwriting is illegible. I told Jon about my problem and the next day he brought home a brand-new **Royal Aristocrat Typewriter.** Notice how I can make some letters darker than others? That feature will come in handy when I need you to hear me yell in print.

Marie, since you are home with your momma,

why didn't you let her pay for postage?
Save every 3 cents you can, girl! You may
want to buy something besides coffee.

Suzy dear, I am so glad you will be
joining these letters, writing our history.
You are only two years younger than Marie,
but you have a different perspective on
everything. You have an old soul inside you.
I knew that each time you recovered from
the hardships you were dealt. For a child
to lose one parent then the second before
the age of ten may not have been uncommon
30 years ago, but it is harder these days.
You do well in school and are thankful for
everything you have. Ethel tells me you
are a hard worker around the house and
practically run the ice cream business in
the afternoons after school. I hope my
children have the stick-to-itiveness that
you do. Maybe we should have a summer camp
run by Suzy and Marie and my children are
the first to attend!

Speaking of children, I have one more
thing to tell you all. I'll leave it till the
end of this letter. To keep your attention.

Jon Jr. is growing too fast. He is only
two years old, but acting like his nearly
five-year-old sister. Yesterday Lelia went
to get him from his crib after a nap, but
something scared her. She came running down
the hall yelling, "Miss Walsh, Jon fell out

of the crib or Lisa got him out. She said when she went in the room, he was on the floor playing with his toys.

Lelia's voice was shaky. She was holding Jon who had a look of pride on his face. Even though I should have been, I was not worried. I knew it wasn't Lisa. She was at a friend's house. Jon looked up at Lelia and laughed. He was bouncing on her hip, like he had just won a prize. Figuring it out, I smiled and said, "Lelia, Lisa's not here. He evidently climbed out himself! Oh my, I don't think we have a baby anymore." I could not help but giggle.

Lelia let herself calm down. Looking at Jon, she warned him about not being so happy with himself. "Well, young'un, if you're old enough to climb, it is time to get you out of those rubber bloomers." Jon thought that was his prize. He bounced in Lelia's arms more eagerly holding his hands up saying, "Rubber boomers, rubber boomers!"

I began chanting, "Rubber bloomers, rubber bloomers, Jon Jon, no more rubber bloomers!" Lelia joined in and by the third verse we were all singing that song.

On reflection, I should not have been so excited. Although Lisa was mostly pantie trained when Jon and I got married, it most likely was not going to be easy with Jon. Thank goodness for Lelia. She often tells me, "Miss Walsh, I have helped raise many young'uns. We can do this."

It reminds me of Momma's favorite saying, "The Nash girls are just fine." I sure am thankful for Lelia.

Seems like every time I am about to get bored, something new comes along. Little Jon is growing up, Lisa will go to school in ten months, and big Jon said he has been asked to take on more duties at the War Department. They plan to bring all branches of the military into offices at the Pentagon. That will take quite an effort on the part of many in the department. Jon says he will lead a team of men to make all that happen. I think if they hired a couple of women, it would be done quickly. With this new job, I will not see him much. I don't see him very often now, but he is able to come home for supper.

Jon wants us to move out of the city. He thinks the schools outside the district will be better for the children. "The suburbs are the place to be," he says. He says that we will get a larger house and a big yard for the children. And because he knew this might win me over, he added, "We will have enough room for your sisters and nieces to come visit anytime you want them here." Okay, that did it. A cure for my boredom and a new project for me to work on.

But you all know how much I love the city. We walk to the park nearly every day. My favorite shops and restaurants are just a few blocks away. There is always something going on, something to do, places to go. Just last week, Jon and I went to a new movie theater called The Palisades to see **A Tree Grows in Brooklyn**. Remember that book by Betty Smith, Caroline? We loved that story and read it out loud to each other when I visited you. They did a good job making it into a movie, but, Caroline, it wasn't the same as the Francie you and I know.

I will be bored to tears in the suburbs. To help change my mind about going, I began thinking about something I don't have in the city but could have in the suburbs. I will buy a car! Since I will need to drive everywhere, I must have a new one. Marie, you will have to help me pick out the next beauty of a car. Please do some research. I want it red and sexy! But it has to fit me and the children. Jon says we can't buy a foreign car. He says that would be unpatriotic. Not sure if there is such a car to fit all my requirements. Finding just the right one will be part of the fun. Since I am cooperating with Jon's idea, I doubt he will care about the cost. Tee hee.

Okay, one big surprise to put at the end

of the letter so you won't stop reading before I end it. I am pregnant again! A new Nash/Walsh child will come in the summer of 1946! I am so excited! Being a mother is my favorite job. And if I do say so myself, I am pretty good at it! I don't care if it's a girl or a boy. I just know if it's a girl, her name will be Dianne. Won't that be wonderful, Suzy?

I am feeling happy/sad with this letter. Tears are falling because we won't see each other this Christmas. But I have to remember we were just together in August. Let's start planning when we will get together sometime soon!

I love you all so much!

Annie

December 26, 1945

Howdy Nash Women!

Yowsa! These letters arrived on Christmas day! The postmaster at Dix tries to get mail to us on special days. It must have arrived on the 24th and they held it to deliver today. Way to time it, Annie! And thanks for still including me.

Doc says I am getting better. I think that means less hard to handle. They still will not give me a job. I am not to be trusted. For two weeks I have been able to walk around the compound and get some exercise. It is cold as a witch's titty in a brass bra, but I like being outside better than inside. It smells so clean in the home. There is a roommate in here that sees bugs and mice, so she cleans all day, every day. Nobody else sees them, and we keep telling her that. The doctors know about it. The nurse says Miss Lois is better than she has ever been. I guess that's why they don't fix the invisible bug problem.

I swear they can fix just about every mental illness here. If they can make me better, they can do it for anyone. I take a fistful of medicine two times a day. You can bet they won't let me skip any of it.

Annie, I was glad to see your children. Thanks for the visit last month. That baby boy doesn't look like a baby any more. And you are going to have another?! What are you thinking? You and Jon do make some pretty children, but isn't two enough?

They don't let me work with the children in the childcare anymore. I can't see Belle's grandchildren either. Annie, your friend Jane explained it to me. I need the medicine and the right kind of treatment to keep me from being psycho. (Of course, she did not use that word.) And when I play with dosage and skip a pill, my brain gets confused, so I make up what is real rather than seeing what is really real. In the case of the Parker children, I forgot that Japan was across the globe. In my defense, they were making a lot of racket near the Parkers' neighborhood. They were building new houses so were dropping trees which was causing great pounding noises. That was even in the newspaper. The neighbors were complaining about it.

I love those children so much. But I can't be trusted. It is not Belle or her son or daughter-in-law that don't trust me with their children. It is the police and the rules of Dix Hill. The children write me a letter or send me a picture nearly every week. They want me to come visit, but I need to wait. I am not sure I can trust myself either.

Dr. Redmond says they will re-evaluate after six months of successful therapy. I have it on my calendar—February 15, 1946. I put an X on every day that goes by. Belle says that is a good way to organize my hopes. In the meantime, there is a lot I have to do.

- Don't mess with my medicine or miss an appointment for anything.
- Do what the housemothers and medical staff tell me to do. Kind of like what Momma would say, don't let laziness get you.
- Exercise and eat well every day.
- Get my work done so I will be a model for the newbies.

Even though I don't have an assigned job, they let me weed the gardens. But there is not much of that to do this time of year. So, they have taught me how to crochet. We tried sewing clothes, but I didn't take to that. If you sew you have to be very careful and particular. When I would mess up, they would make me pull out a long line of stitches and do it again. That made me mad, and I was not so nice about it. They stopped making me do it because, as Momma would say, they were "trying to get a silk purse out of a sow's ear."

Guess what you all are getting for Christmas? A crocheted something! I have patterns to make a cover for the couch, a collar, handbags, and table covers. Most of these things make no sense. If I learn to knit, I can make everyone some mittens. Now that can be useful.

I want to learn how to cook. At my last weekly meeting with Dr. Redmond, I asked if I could apply for a kitchen job. You all know how calm that man is, but I don't think he liked that idea because his eyes got wide and he crossed his arms. After a very long pause, he said, "Well that's an idea. We will talk next week about what that type of work entails." In other words—NO.

Later that night in bed, I realized it might scare him to let me use a knife. They don't give us residents knives with our meals.

Ethel, please come visit soon. I need a Nash hug. I need you to tell me about your life as a business woman and boss lady. Annie came in December. It is your turn in January. Okay?

One more thing. I thank you for loving me. I am not an easy person, but you put up with me. Someday

I will love myself just as much as you love me.

Caroline

p.s. I am sending this to Suzy.
She can give it to Ethel.

December 29, 1945

Dear Aunties, Mothers, and all the rest,

I am so excited to be included in these letters. So is my teacher at school. When I told her about this, she said I must write in my best cursive. She said people love to read cursive because it is a beautiful style. She began practicing with me after school in early December so I would get the idea of not picking the pen from the paper until the end of a word. The problem is it takes a long time to make the words just right. I probably won't write very long letters.

In October I turned 16 years old. I feel like that is nearly middle aged. One reason is I can no longer wear hand-me-downs from Marie. Our sizes are about the same and with Marie away at college, I don't have the shared clothes at home. Momma and Daddy Larry have to buy clothes for me. I get to pick them out of the Sears Roebuck catalog, but it is hard to get the right fit from a picture. Miss Alta, who lives down the street, is teaching me to stitch up the clothes so they fit. Another reason I feel older than I want to be is everyone thinks I should have a boyfriend. Boys are not who I want to hang out with. They are mean and hateful. So, I ignore them. Daddy Larry says I will change my mind soon enough. I don't think so.

Here are my thank yous for Christmas gifts. This way I won't have to write separate letters.

Caroline, I love the crocheted handbag. At first, I wasn't sure why I needed it, but now I figured out I should carry a couple of pieces of paper, a pencil, and the key to the house. Those fit just right in that handbag. Thank you, Caroline!

Annie, thank you for the Life Magazine. It is like a text book of worldly things. I read it from cover to cover as soon as it arrives in the mail. Then I pass it around to my friends to read. I am becoming so sophisticated with that knowledge.

Marie, I have already thanked you, but I'll do it again here. More cursive practice is good for me. The sweater you sent in NC State College colors is terrific—red with white buttons! The best. I wear it nearly every day!

Momma, you know how much I love the gift you gave me. Like these letters, this gift will help me create a history of this family and my life. For those that don't know, Daddy Larry helped Momma pick out an Argus camera so I can take 35mm pictures. It has a strap so I can wear it around my neck with or without its brown leather case. It is divine! When we are all together again, I want to take a family picture of all the Nash girls and boys.

My hand is tired, so I will stop for now.

Love you bunches!

Suzy Dixon Nash

January 11, 1946

Happy New Year, family!

1946 has happened! YAY! I need a new year to come. The world needs 1945 to be gone! I actually burned that calendar in the fireplace last week. Good riddance!

It took me a while to get around to writing my letter. Now with telephones, I talk to y'all and am not sure what else I should write. Suzy and I were so excited when the letters arrived addressed to her that we both sat down and read them that day. Last night I read hers.

I must say she did an uppity good job with her penmanship. I officially name her the writer of wedding invitations, baby announcements, graduations, and all things that we want to make us look fancy. You can pay her by the note, and she will drop it in her savings account. Tee hee.

Well, Larry did not make it home for Christmas, and he's in the dog house for it! That man has always liked traveling, but I thought since he's now a married man, he would come home for Christmas!! He calls me nearly every night, but that is not the same as having him here. He better bring something great when he arrives. I told him I could use a new pair of shoes since I was doing all the work around here. My comfy shoes are wearing out on the bottom. Last night he said he'd be back at the end of the month on Sunday, January 27th.

Caroline, I have made plans to come see you next weekend January 18th. Suzy will ride with me, and we will visit Marie if she can make room in her busy school life. I will call Dix Hill tomorrow to arrange for us to stay in one of the guest houses for two nights. I like staying near you when we visit. You get to show us everything new that you are doing, and we get to eat together. Just like in the old days. Suzy and I are bringing the second half of your Christmas present. Annie and I chipped in together to get it for you. It will finish up the surprise. For those that don't know, I sent a music book to Caroline before Christmas so she can learn to read music. Not sure how that works, but it was on her list.

Now that the war is over, business is picking up. Men are coming home to wives who are too busy to do the laundry. That makes more for me and Suzy to do. I'm finding out that the men don't always know that the womenfolk are sending the laundry out to get done. When Mary Jo Smith came to pick up her laundry last week, she asked me to keep the washing and pressing of her husband's clothes a secret. She said her Johnny thinks she does it all. But when the couples get together to play cards, some are starting to wag their tongues about how hard it is to get it all done with the men back home. Mary Jo said one of men told the others that there is no way the laundry is getting done at home. According to MaryJo, the husband said, "I know she ain't doing the clothes. We don't even own a washing machine!"

I said to Mary Jo, "Do you want me to keep a secret about how you have me do the laundry, or are you gonna buy a washing machine and rig up a clothes line?"

She leaned in closer and whispered, "Heck, Ethel, I am not doing his nasty drawers! And I don't want him to know who does."

Right then and there, I told Suzy we need to go up in our prices in the new year. Keeping secrets cost extra. I'm even thinking about buying a dozen or so household washing machines at a discount price. I can store them out back and sell them at a premium price to the women who can't keep the secret anymore.

I think 1946 is going to be my year for building up my financial nest! Like you, Annie, I don't want to live in the suburbs, but I would like to live in a house that is not behind the backwall of three gas dryers and five electric washing machines going all day.

Caroline, when we talked about starting the round-robin letters up again, at first you said you were not going to write. You really didn't want to read the letters either, as you said, "about everyone's glorious life but yours." Don't forget my glorious life includes men and women's dirty drawers!

I think you did a good job on your letter. We like knowing what's up with you, and I like that you make us laugh. I remember that first round of letters you were only 14 or so. You cracked me up about catching that Walker boy having a go-around with Mrs. Murphy on the kitchen table. And you had the Murphy children in tow! I was sure proud of how you stood up to that boy when he wanted you to lie for him.

Let's keep trying to see the funny side of this nutty world. I can't wait for my crocheted collar. What the heck is that anyway? If that becomes a thing, I don't think I will know how to wash it.

Marie, you and I talked about Frank's last visit, but I had not told the rest of the group. Skip the next few pages if you don't want to hear it again.

Y'all know that Frank and Elizabeth got married in July. Well evidently it was a shotgun wedding because Elizabeth must have been already pregnant. They're expecting the child in a few months. Frank came by to tell me and Marie just before Christmas. I'm not sure why, but I got emotional about that. Even though Frank hasn't been in my life for many years, I got mad about him being a father with someone but me. It's inevitable, I guess. I worried about how

Marie was going to take the news. But she took it better than me.

In early December, with the regular Christmas card Frank sends every year, he had a separate note just to me. When he sends something like that, it used to mean he was going to ask me to come back and be his wife. Plus he sends money. I think it's a form of bribery. But this time the letter was different. Here is the content in a nutshell.

He reminded me that he and E (how dare he call her E!) got married in July. He said he'd not seen Marie in many months and wanted to come by for a visit and let me meet Elizabeth. Marie, of course, had met her, but I hadn't gotten around to it.

He said he would like to come by the week before Christmas and asked if we were available.

He said he was bringing a different kind of Christmas present that needed to be delivered in person. I figured he was bringing Marie another car.

With a quick rehash of his life and how he loved me from the moment we met—and so on and so on—he said he would always love me and that Marie was one of the most important things in his life. I wondered what MRS. FRANK POLLARD thinks about that.

He said he would arrive with her on December 22nd. I knew I would not want her to come. We did not need to set a new version of Christmas with MRS. E!

After reading my letter from him, I called Frank and told him he could come on the 22nd but not with Elizabeth. I tried to be nice, and you know how hard that is for me. I told him it would be more special to hear any news that affected Marie without the new wife.

Marie was on break from college, so she was home on the 22nd. Suzy was home too, but she had gone to visit friends. Suzy has never been a Frank fan. She told Marie she would catch up later on any news.

Marie and I made BLT sandwiches. Marie knew it was one of his favorites because every time they go out to lunch, he tells her that. I also knew he liked fried okra, so we made that too. And of course, dessert would be a banana split. We sell them every day in the summer but only have the ingredients every now and then in the winter.

I remember the first time Marie and Suzy made banana splits for the customers. They watched me closely when I did it for a whole week. Luckily two customers came to the window and asked for two banana splits. I called the girls in and tested their knowledge. "Each of you write down the recipe for a real Kooler banana split, and if you get it right, you get your first chance doing it on your own."

The customer overheard and objected, "Hey, I don't want a first-time banana split! I hear they are the best made ice cream dessert in all of North Carolina. I am buying one for my new girlfriend. It's gotta be right!"

My reply was simple. "Don't worry, sir, I invented the best banana split recipe in all of North Carolina. I'll oversee the production. And if you say you don't like it, well, you'd be lying, but I'll still let you go along your way."

He smiled knowing darn well it would be delicious. He called his girlfriend to come to the window to watch how we make a Kooler banana split.

Marie and Suzy went to the kitchen table and wrote one recipe together. They did a perfect job complete with smart aleck comments. I still have it today.

Kooler Banana Split – the best in North Carolina

Use the paper cup shaped like a banana boat

Slice one banana in half – long ways. Lay each piece flat down in the boat. That means round side up.

Put one scoop of vanilla ice cream on top on the right side.

One scoop of chocolate ice cream on the left side.

One scoop of strawberry ice cream in the middle.

Using one spoonful of Momma's sweet walnut syrup, spread across all three flavors of ice cream. "Not too much, money doesn't grow on trees you know."

Whisk whipped cream again. It gets made every morning and will need "a little fluff."

One dollop of whipped cream on the top of each flavor of ice cream.

One maraschino cherry on the top of each mound of whipped cream.

Give only one napkin and one spoon per split except if two people are sharing.

Each of you know all the other recipes from the summers visiting here. If you stay more than a few days, you have to pitch in. Maybe I should have each of you write down the way to make all the famous Kooler ice cream delights! We can make a book out of it and sell it to those that want to own a Kooler Ice Cream Shop. Maybe I can get a percentage of every delight they sell.

Caroline, you write the recipe for your favorite—the hot fudge sundae.

Annie, you can teach your children the correct way to dip a cone of vanilla into the chocolate that hardens right away. Remember the trick is coating the edge of the cone and using the right wrist action.

I can write the ingredients for the pineapple sundae and what's needed to make the three flavors of ice cream.

Back to the point I was trying to make. Frank visited without Elizabeth. He brought a large picnic basket filled with food. There was a Virginia cured ham, plenty of potatoes, turnips, fresh picked and shelled butter beans, and a huge bowl of Ambrosia.

"Ethel, I know you were making sandwiches for today. I am looking forward to that. I thought I'd bring some things for your Christmas dinner. Remember Ambrosia? Your momma taught me how to make it with marshmallows and cherries. 'The food of the gods,' she used to say."

My chest filled up with my heart. I certainly do remember. Thank you, Frank.

"Marie, this is a typical Christmas dinner when we were young. I don't think I have made Ambrosia for you."

Frank looked at me like he was trying to flirt. I looked away, taking the food to the cupboard. He stepped over to Marie, took the top off the bowl of Ambrosia and put it up to her nose. "Marie, smell that. After you taste this you will want to have it all the time."

We sat at the small table to have lunch. Marie served her daddy's plate. To move from small talk about the drive down from Virginia and how Marie was liking school, I said "Frank, what brings you here? What's on your mind?"

Those blue eyes watched me as I poured the iced tea in his glass. He was still a handsome man. "Marie, Ethel, I am happy to tell you that Elizabeth is with child. We are expecting a baby in the spring. I wanted you to know. Marie will have another sister."

I quickly interrupted, "Half-sister."

"Ethel, no matter. I am Marie's father, and I want to bring our families together. That is why I wanted to bring Elizabeth to announce this news with me. What would make us the happiest is that we gather at special times for the rest of our lives. Neither you nor I have parents anymore. But we should have an extended family. Wouldn't it be grand to have Easter with all the Nash children and grandchildren hunting Easter eggs? Just imagine Thanksgiving with Annie's family, Caroline's friends and future family, yours and mine around the table enjoying each other and being thankful together."

Now sisters and our children, I wanted to write this in a letter rather than telling you about it on the telephone. It will give you time to think about it. Frank's request involves y'all. We know Frank and I will not get back together. We have moved on from our childhood. But I'm trying to imagine having a bigger family. The Nash sisters are fine people. Maybe we need to rub off on the next generation.

We will talk more about this later.

I love you bunches,

Ethel

CHAPTER 7 — MARCH 1, 1946

Annie
Double in Size

I HAVE NEVER BEEN SO scared in all my life.

I love being pregnant, and giving birth to Jon Jr. was not a big deal. He was 7 pounds 6 ounces and came only a few days later than expected. The birthing process went along as Ethel had said it would. She only gave birth once, but she said she knew what she was doing when our sister Dianne had Suzy. She claims she is an expert.

Going to the doctor with Jon for a regular check-up was no biggie. I knew it would be a short visit. He would just feel my swelling belly, listen to what was going on inside, and calculate a due date. Just as with Jon Jr. In fact, this was so routine, Jon and I decided to go for a late lunch afterward. These days I couldn't eat just anything, so we planned to go to our tried and true place—Ebbitt Grill on 15th Street NW. I had a craving for their spaghetti with meatballs. At least I hope what I was feeling was a craving.

But this appointment turned out not to be routine. I was on the exam table; Jon was standing beside my shoulder. As the doctor moved his stethoscope around on my belly, he make a curious "huh" sound under his breath. He moved it again and made that same sound. Jon and I looked at the doctor's face. "What does that mean?" Jon calmly asked.

"Just a moment, Mr. Walsh. Let me try again."

It seemed like he had touched my lower body everywhere possible then announced, "Well, I think we have two healthy babies in there."

I shouted, "Good God almighty—help me! Two! Are you sure, doctor? Absolutely certain?" I grabbed Jon's hand, wondering how that could be possible.

Jon almost passed out. His face lost its color. Because his legs went limp, the doctor guided him to a chair. I was a bit perturbed by that. He is not having these babies—I am!

Seeming to be a bit offended, the doctor spoke to me, "Yes, I'm certain. There are two heartbeats there. I'm not mistaken because each has a distinct rhythm."

Then addressing Jon, he said, "It will be just fine, Mr. Walsh. Healthy women do this all the time."

The color that had left Jon moved over to me. My face was heating up like I was standing in front of a furnace. "Good grief, Jon. Get over it. Don't forget who's giving birth to two babies at once!"

I wanted to know when the babies were coming, but more importantly I wanted to know how that was possible. The doctor evidently heard my thoughts and explained, "Miss Walsh, they don't come out at exactly the same time. One is usually a few minutes behind the other. You are about six months along. We want the babies to stay right where they are to develop as much as they can. We will be watching them very closely. I think they will be ready to greet you in June or so. I know you had your first child with a mid-wife at home, but this time I will be with you at a hospital."

I looked at Jon and felt all alone. With my voice shaking and the tone loud, I commanded, "Jon, call Ethel and tell her to come right away!"

He was finally able to speak. "Annie darling, she doesn't need to come right away. The babies will not be here for months."

"Jon, call her to come or I will get in the car and drive to her. I need my sister!"

The doctor stepped toward the door and opened it without even looking at Jon. We knew it was a message. Jon left the room.

The doctor came over to me, put his hand on my shoulder, and said, "Miss Walsh, we will work together to bring these babies healthy and happy out to see their mother. I'll see you every two weeks. We'll monitor you and these children closely."

I nodded my head at the doctor as he stepped out of the room. Lying back on the table, I began breathing more rhythmically. I felt a bit guilty about being mean to Jon. But dang it, he really has no idea what I need! My sister will know. She will help me find the confidence to endure this. I pulled myself from the table, washed up, pulled on my clothes, and went out the door. Jon was sitting in the waiting room—NOT making a phone call!

"Is Ethel coming?"

Without raising his eyes to me and almost in a whisper, he said, "I could not reach her. No one answered the telephone. We can try again when we get home. But I want us to talk about this sensibly before you call."

Stomping my feet, I went out the office door. I stepped outside and raised my hand for a taxi. As one pulled up quickly, I turned and said, "You go to lunch without me, Jon. I am going home. I need to be alone to process this catastrophe!"

The taxi pulled away with Jon looking rejected and clueless. I knew his driver would come along shortly and carry that little boy to wherever he wanted to go.

It was nearly dinner time when Jon came shuffling and stumbling into the house. I was in the living room trying once more to reach Ethel. Where in the heck was she anyway?

Jon came over to me, leaning way too much for a sober man and nearly fell on me. I pushed him away, but he persisted. Slurring his words next to my face he said, "My shweet Annie. Aren't ya happy? We are gonna have twosh babies at once. It might hurt like crap, but you are the schrongest woman I know. You will bring two beautiful babies into thish world. I can't do it for you, but I will be right there when the doctor will let me."

I stood up from the couch, and he fell over on his side. I was still holding the telephone waiting to see if

Ethel would pick up. I laid down the receiver and left the room for the kitchen telephone.

As I put the receiver to my ear, I heard Jon saying, "Heello, Heello, Ethel girl."

"Hello yourself," said Ethel on the other end of the line. "Is this Jon? Are you drunk? What are y'all celebrating?"

I yelled both into the other room and into the receiver, "Jon, hang up the darn telephone!"

"Ouch my ears, sister. What is going on?" Ethel almost screamed back.

As I heard the click of the ear piece being placed back on its resting place, I was about to cry.

"Sister, I need you."

Before she could respond, I kept on, "Can you come to Washington? I can pay for the train ride or the gasoline. Or maybe I should come to see you. Except I don't want to leave the children with my dang husband. My life is about to change drastically! I need my sister. The doctors really don't know what it is like. Nobody really understands. Jon thinks he knows everything! But this is not happening to him!"

Ethel tried to interrupt several times, and finally she got through with her loud Ethel tone. "Whoa, Annie! Slow down, girl! What the heck is happening? Doctors? Are you sick? Take five long slow breaths, and then I will listen to you. Calm it, girl!"

I moved the receiver to the other ear and focused on my breathing. After the fourth breath, I was able to sit down and remove my hand from my hair. Ethel often bargained her way into getting me to behave.

"Okay, I'm calm. Are you sitting down? You know I am having a baby, right? Well, it is not a baby—it's two babies! I went to the doctor this morning, and he hears two heartbeats. Oh lord, how am I going to carry two babies?"

Ethel moved into momma mode. "Annie, women have twins all the time. Well, not all the time, but it is common. Is the doctor worried about you being able to carry them?"

"That is exactly what the doctor said—'Women do this all the time.' But not me. How on earth am I going to have two babies come through my you-know-what? How am I going to be able to stand up with that much weight on me?"

"Okay, I get it. But I carry the weight of three extra babies around my gut all the time. You adjust. And always wear comfortable shoes." Of course, she made me laugh.

Ethel continued, "What do you need me for right now? When are the babies due? That is when you will need me, Lelia, Jon, and everybody."

I told the rest of the story and even more than I should by telephone. "The doctor thinks they will be big enough to deliver by early June. He said not to worry about my weight because I will be eating for three now. Oh geez, I will be as big as a house. Ethel, you are the expert with birthing babies, I need you here with me. Jon will be no good. He turned white as a sheet and nearly fell on the floor when the doctor told us the news. Anyway, he is never around here to help. So, I can't count on him. Oh yeah, the doc said he wants to monitor the babies every two weeks. The babies? What about me?" I could feel my muscles tightening with the stress of it all. Ethel must have noticed through the telephone wire.

"Annie, relax. I will come for a visit so we can talk through this. But you will not need me for the next many months. And I can't leave the business with Larry that long. Get your rich husband to organize me a train trip from Raleigh, and I can stop by to see Caroline on the way. Larry is not scheduled to drive for another month or so. He can manage things here. Now hold on and let me find a calendar. You go get one too."

We set the date for Friday. Ethel would drive to Raleigh, visit Caroline, and catch the afternoon train. If all went as planned, she would arrive before bedtime. Ethel said she could stay a few days, depending on how things went. Leaning back, I allowed my whole, soon to be gigantic, body to fill the kitchen chair. "Oh, Ethel, thank you so much. I am still scared out of my wits, but I know nothing bad is going to happen before Saturday. I will have the guest room made up for my favorite sister."

"Well, you don't have a lot of sisters to choose from and I doubt Caroline can help with birthing babies, so I'm your favorite right now. I have a few things for you to remember. First, if the doctor is monitoring the babies every two weeks, you can bet he is checking on the mother that is holding them. And second, start a diary of how you are feeling. Write in it every day. You probably will not see huge day-to-day changes until closer to the due date. Take the diary to your appointments with your doctor so you won't forget to ask him questions. And there's more—of course, Jon can be no help with pregnancy. No man can. But he loves you. Talk to him about staying home more as those babies get big and want to come out. And tell him I said to stop drinking so much. And he better not say I am the pot calling the kettle black. I'm not the one having a huge responsibility coming. Most of all, Annie, you are a Nash woman. You are smart and strong. Don't give into fear. Just think what we all have gone through. This will be a piece of coconut cake!

"Now hang up the telephone and tell your husband you are sorry for being mean. Like you told me once, 'Acting stupid does not help us reach our goals in life.'"

By this time, I was nearly crying. Not from stress or fear but from love of family. Yes, I can manage two more children with that.

I heard the click of an ended conversation and noticed Jon standing behind me. He put his hand on my shoulder and said just the right thing, "What can I do to help, darling?"

Chapter 8 — March 15, 1946

Ethel
Family Is Everywhere

I DROVE TO SEE CAROLINE. Spring is a good time to drive, especially alone. I rolled down all the windows, turned up the radio, and sang as loud as I wanted. On my list of sing-a-long music is what we used to listen to as teenagers on the radio at home. It never matters who sings the songs just as long as they don't change too much from the original. When the car radio didn't play the songs I wanted to hear, I turned it off and sang those songs by myself.

I didn't want to forget what songs came to mind so I could get Annie to sing with me. I pulled over for a minute and wrote them down. Annie and I gave Caroline the sheet music to some of them for Christmas. We also gave her a guitar to teach herself to play. Maybe that'll cut down on the crocheted items we will get as presents. And maybe we can sing the next time we're all together at Dix Hill.

Here's what I wrote down:

Happy Days Are Here Again – This is the Nash Family favorite because some days are not happy.

Puttin' on the Ritz – This reminds me of staying in that fancy hotel in Raleigh.

Let Me Sing & I'm Happy – Like #1

Dancing on the Ceiling – This was our teenage Saturday night song. Plenty of dancing with it.

Somewhere over the Rainbow – One that always makes us cry.

You're Driving Me Crazy! – Caroline says we drive her crazy.

We believed we were The Nash Sister Singers—Annie, Caroline, Dianne and me. Dianne and I would make up our own words to songs sometimes. Singing took our mind off crazy.

I drove through the gates of Dix Hill. I appreciate that they do a good job keeping up the land for those that have to work here, live here, and visit family. No one is at Dix Hill without a sad story, but coming on the property this time of year brings a little happiness. Spring leaves were just starting to burst through the bare branches of the oak trees. Raleigh has more oak trees than anywhere I've lived. They make good shade, which we need in the South. Forsythia was showing off its yellow dress. I could see that daffodils were, as Momma used to call it, crowning. Their skinny green leaves were coming out of the winter ground.

Pulling toward the small office where they check people coming and going, I got in the long line of cars waiting to drive through. I guess it was change of shift time for the workers or more visitors than usual. Caroline had let them know I was coming, so it won't take but a few minutes once I get to the front of the line.

It was my turn. I could see the large Negro man who is always there. Mr. Jones has a smile that makes everyone feel welcome, "Hello, Mrs. Ethel Martin! Bless you for coming to visit. How was your drive up this morning?"

"Well howdy, Mr. Jones. It was a lovely drive. Spring is coming. A good time to see North Carolina. I hope things are serving you well. What's with the crowd?"

Relaxing that smile a bit, Mr. Jones replied. "It's a big visiting day. There have been a lot of new people coming to stay in the last few weeks, and today their families are visiting. I like seeing families come to visit. Sometimes those living here don't have families who visit."

As he was writing on the papers to get me checked in, I tried to bring that smile back, "Well, Mr. Jones, that's something my family calls a sad/happy occasion. Sad because the people are struggling without family that can visit and happy because this is such a good place to get help with those struggles. They will get better with all the people like you who can be their family. We appreciate you, Mr. Jones."

The beaming smile came back. He nodded his head, and he waved his hand at me to allow me through. "Bless you, Mrs. Martin. Now go hug that sister of yours."

I waved back, pushing away the sad reality of what

was here and trying to believe what I said.

I pulled in front of the house Caroline had described. They let her move out of the hospital and back into one of the group homes. Caroline once said that they let people do that when they can live together without losing it on each other. When I called Caroline a few days ago, she was talking a mile a minute about her six roommates. "I can't wait for you to see my new digs. I'm in one of the newer houses. It reminds me of home—painted white with a front porch and three bedrooms. As soon as they let me, I'm gonna plant some yellow roses." When she told me that, my throat swelled up. That was Momma's favorite flower. Daddy planted them along a fence for her at the home place.

Evidently Caroline had been watching out for me. Before I could cut the motor, she came running out the front door. Even though she's nearly thirty years old, I saw a teenager in the way she near skipped toward the car. She was waving one hand high in the air. "Hey there, big sister!" she yelled. "Finally, you came to see me." As if I never did.

I blinked. That didn't look like a person who is so confused about reality she can endanger children. Was I seeing things? There was my young sister. An innocent girl with the world in front of her.

And here is the funny thing. Caroline was in a dress with a black fitted bodice and white skirt covered in colorful applique. The skirt was gathered so full, it would swing when she walked. She was wearing some fancy black Oxford shoes. I knew what they were called because Marie asked for a pair for Christmas.

Caroline's hair was pinned back on one side behind her ear and wavy on the other side. She looked like a model in a magazine. I squinted to make sure that was really my sister.

As she approached me, I yelled back, "Well, look at you! Are you meeting the queen today? As Annie would say, you look smashing!"

She raised her hand to almost touch her hair. Her palm shaped the style of the do. She turned round and round, so the hem of the dress whirled out around her knees. I noticed that she was even wearing earrings. Oh geez, had she stolen something?

I took her in my arms and received her big hug. Goodness, when did she shrink? I am the shortest in the family. What the heck? "Caroline, you do look smashing. How are you feeling?"

I could only think they had her on some new medicine.

"Ethel, I am better than I have ever been. Dr. Redmond has adjusted my medication, and I never knew I could feel so normal." BINGO, I thought. "And guess what? I have a beau!"

I almost fell to the ground. She had to hold me up. "Caroline, let's go sit down. A beau? I think I want to hear all about it."

That phrase is one the doctor taught us to say. "Don't question when she expresses her reality," he said. "Just say you want to hear about it." But I was feeling sick to my stomach. I am not sure I want to hear about it.

Caroline and I spent a while in rocking chairs on

the front porch of her home. That's what she called it, although I was a bit offended. Our home is where we grew up. Every other place we live is just a new house. She explained that she met someone that lives on the Dix Hill campus. Campus—another word I had not heard. Maybe they were teaching them to think they were in college.

She told me about this person named Joe. Although a common name, I couldn't help but remember that Dianne's husband, Suzy's daddy, was Joe. Caroline said Joe lives on the other side of the campus, and she met him at the dances they put on once a month. To shock my system, she added, "And we've been courtin'."

My mind was swirling like her skirt. Dances. Courting. Joe. Beau. Holy cow! I gotta get to Dr. Redmond!

After taking a deep breath and trying not to look as shocked as I felt, I asked, "Caroline, what is courtin'?"

"That, sister, is a stupid question. You know what courtin' is. You had a baby with Frank. Before babies is courtin'. You know holding, kissing, touching, and stuff."

I was about to faint. Until I could get to Dr. Redmond, I needed to stop talking about this. To change the subject, I said, "Oh Caroline, you know I am going to Washington to see Annie. But I didn't have a chance to tell you why. You know she is pregnant from the last group of round-robin letters. Well, the big news is that she is pregnant with twins. Isn't that something?"

Caroline did not want to hear it. "Aren't you happy for me, Ethel? I am seeing a man. Just like normal folks. And before you even try to stop it, Dr. Redmond knows. Nurse Joanna said it is healthy to care about someone else."

I could barely breathe. "You care about lots of people! Annie, me, Belle, and her grandchildren. And your whole family!"

"Family?" she asked. "My family is here. I have lived more years here than around any of y'all. You visit, and I like it. A lot. Many people here never have anyone visit. But visitors are not family. Joe and I can be family. Nurse Joanna is family. Belle is family. And even Dr. Mark."

Dr. Mark, I thought. Way too friendly if you ask me. I needed to walk. Actually, I wanted to run straight to the doctor's office. My mind took me to what Momma might do right now. It seemed she was never shocked or given to a hissy fit. I decided I needed some thinking time.

"Caroline, let's take a walk. I need to take in these changes. Can you walk with me to the picnic tables under the oaks over there?"

It was about a half mile. If I could make it without passing out from the exercise or the stress of my sister with mental issues having a boyfriend, it would give me some time to figure out what to say next. Geez, where are my sisters when I need them? I talk better with others around thinking with me.

"Okay, Ethel. We can do that. But you are not going to out talk me about any of this. I am happier than I have been all my life. I was excited to tell you. Don't make this a thing!" Her eyes were focused on me like she wanted to spit.

The air got cold. I decided I needed a coat. Walking to the car to grab my jacket, I suggested she might need one too. "Do you need a sweater or something, Caroline? There is a chill in the air."

Her expression changed quickly from an angry stare to a wide smile. She turned and dashed to the house yelling back to me, "I'll get my sweater. Then I can tell you all about dreamy Joe and me."

Oh, good lord. Is this because of the new medicine? Is this a lapse of reality? Is she just pulling my leg? Or is it real? I could tell right then I'd have to catch a later train to Washington.

I really did not need to prepare questions to pull out the details. Caroline began talking for what seemed like another hour and didn't slow down once. She described Joe, how they "fell in love," and the counseling that had happened with Dr. Redmond about her "love life." She talked about her walks with Joe around the campus every few days, what they talked about, and that holding hands made her stomach get butterflies. The whole time she was smiling and giggling and often getting up from the bench to add drama to her words. Evidently spinning in her skirt was the way to enlighten me about what love looks like.

Pushing down the bile I felt coming up from my stomach, I stood up from the bench and put one hand on Caroline's shoulder to slow her down. "Sister, I am glad you are happy. But all this makes me nervous. I don't want you to be hurt. You've never really showed interest in a boy. Now all of a sudden you are in love. I don't think it happens that way in normal times. With the way your life has been, I am surprised this is happening so fast."

Caroline stopped spinning and slammed herself down on the bench. She gave me that cow-eyed look that usually makes me want to rescue her. To avoid the begging eyes, I got up and went to stand behind her. I wrapped my arms around her, clutching her shoulders. I was checking to feel any fear or tremors in her. There was nothing but stillness and breathing. I rested my head on her back and said, "Give me some time to get used to this, baby girl. Then you will see how happy I can be for you. Can you do that?"

She nodded her head and turned in my arms to finish the hug. "Okay, big sister, I will wait for you to get used to it. But I am not gonna stop seeing Joe. He pleases me so."

We walked back to Caroline's house hand in hand like Momma would have. Caroline was humming a song and swinging our clasped hands, which we Nash sisters did often. She began humming "Jesus Loves Me" loudly. At that moment, she was my ten-year-old sister. I hummed along as if it was twenty years ago.

I got another big Nash sister hug, and I told her I would come see her on my way back from Annie's house. Caroline walked slowly into her house, not looking back but swishing her skirt as she moved.

I could not leave Dix Hill before I talked to Dr. Redmond or Nurse Joanna. I wanted to know if what Caroline is saying is real. If it is, there are real worries. If it's not, then the medical staff needs to know.

I drove over to the main hospital building, parked in front, and nearly ran through the entrance hall to speak to the reception lady.

In my don't-mess-with-me voice I said, "I must see Dr. Redmond. I just visited my sister, and I'm very worried about her!"

The receptionist rose from her chair, "I am sorry, but Dr. Redmond has gone for the day. Tell me your name and what is bothering your sister, then I can find the right person for you to talk to."

"Okay, then get Nurse Joanna Dunn, she knows me and my sister very well. I am Ethel Martin and Caroline Nash is running around with a man. I need to know if that is real or if she is having another break from reality. She is not well. If she does have a boyfriend she could get pregnant. Boyfriend my eye, it would be a man who might be taking advantage of her. My sister cannot have a baby!"

As calm as these people are, I had her attention now. Her eyes got big and round, and she moved to the front of her desk. She looked around to see who might be hearing me. In nearly a whisper, she said "Mrs. Martin, can you lower your voice? Have a seat and let me get Nurse Dunn. I know she is here. I just saw her walk down the hall."

As the woman signaled which hall, I took off running. Well, as much as I can run. It actually was a fast walk in that direction.

"Mrs. Martin, wait. I can get her for you. Please stay here." Hearing her voice fade behind me didn't stop me. But heavy footsteps of a man coming after me slowed me down a bit. I never knew they had guards in the building. But out of the blue, there he was. "Madam, you must stop!" he boomed.

I stopped fast as if the next step would throw me into a pit of snakes. The guard grabbed my arm to gain control. I didn't think I should fight him. He was way bigger than me.

By then the commotion had caused a gathering in the hallway where I was headed. One of the people noticing the ruckus was Joanna Dunn. Doing a double step, she came quickly. As she got close enough to see me, she said, "Mrs. Martin, is that you? I looked down the hall and thought I saw Caroline. Are you okay? How can I help?"

She thanked the guard and the approaching crowd, "It's okay everyone. This is Ethel Martin. She is a family member of one of our residents. Everyone, you can go back to work."

The guard let go of my arm but didn't step away. He was there to protect Nurse Dunn from me, I guess.

I calmed myself and acted as civil as I could. "I am sorry to create such as an uproar. Nurse Joanna, can I speak with you? I just visited Caroline, and she told me some disturbing things."

"Of course, Mrs. Martin. Let's step into this office over here." She shifted her gaze from my face to the guard. "Mr. Wilder, I will be fine with Mrs. Martin. Thank you for your assistance."

I followed her into what seemed to be a small classroom. We both sat down. Nurse Joanna grabbed one of the pads of paper and a pencil from the table.

As I began talking, her hand moved fast writing something on the paper that looked like gibberish. I tried to read what she was writing, but none of the words were legible. She paused and turned the paper toward me.

"Short hand," she said. "It helps me write fast when people talk. I will translate this back to writing that you are able to read."

"Oh, okay. My sister Annie knows how to do that. She used to work in the War Department in Washington, DC. Evidently those men talk real fast too." I had no idea why I was telling her this.

To get me back on track, she asked, "Mrs. Martin, how was Caroline at your visit today?"

I started again almost without a breath between sentences. I knew she could keep up.

"It was outrageous! She acted like a teenager, and she was wearing fancy clothes and had her hair done up professionally. Where did she get those clothes? She doesn't have access to her money here. Does she? And she went on and on about her boyfriend, Joe. She told me what he looks like, how good he dances, and how they are courting! I'm hoping this is all made up, but I'm worried it is not. She can't have a boyfriend! Can she? She's not well. How is she going to handle this? Why did y'all let her see men?"

Nurse Joanna paused, put down her pencil, and placed her hands on the paper she had been writing on. She was probably trying to get me to stop talking about such silliness. I hope.

In her nurse tone, she tried to slow me down a bit.

"Mrs. Martin, it sounds like this upset you. Was Caroline also upset?"

"Yes, I am worried, and I told Caroline so, but I was not as frantic as I am now. She didn't seem upset except when she asked me why I was not happy for her. I think she is living in a made-up world. And if she is, that is not normal either. Right? Maybe y'all need to adjust her meds. And if this is real, she needs to be isolated from men."

The more I talked the more agitated I was. I decided I should take a few deep breaths.

"Oh, I see. The fact that she might have a friend who is a man is worrisome," Nurse Joanna said with a technique they taught us to use with Caroline—reflect back what you heard and validate their feelings. "Why does that worry you?"

I placed my hands on the table quietly and calmly. My answer was slower as I was processing what I heard. "Oh SUGAR! Does that mean this is true? If it is, I'm worried. Very worried. Caroline is not really thirty years old. In her ability to understand reality, to make decisions, she is more like fifteen. She can't do things with a man. And most of all she can't get pregnant!"

There was the truth tumbling out from my heart through my mouth. "I had a baby as a teenager with a man who did not love me enough to hang around and be the daddy. It was hard, but I had sisters and a momma to help. Caroline lives in an asylum. She can't take care of a baby. What if he breaks her heart like mine was broken? She won't endure that."

There were several minutes of silence between us. Nurse Joanna was no longer writing, just listening. Her face gave away no emotion. Then she presented a solution. "How long will you be staying in Raleigh? Dr. Redmond will be back on Monday. He will be able to talk about what you might be feeling."

"Nurse Joanna, we've got another crisis in this family right now. I am on my way to my sister Annie's house in Washington, DC. That also is important. I am leaving on the train tonight, and once things calm down there, I am planning to come back next week. I can meet with Dr. Redmond then. Let's say Tuesday." I needed to get to the real point, so I continued, "What is the bottom line? Is Caroline seeing reality? Does she have a man-friend?"

Again, she moved into psychology-careful mode. "Ethel—may I call you that?" I nodded. It didn't really matter. "Ethel, I do not know the details as well as Dr. Redmond does. He meets weekly with Caroline for counseling. She trusts him, so I believe she is being honest with him, and he with her. Most of what you have told me verifies reality. We do hold co-ed dances a couple of times a month. Both music and interactions with others are part of therapy for our patients. Joe is a friend to Caroline. Women and men are allowed to date one another once the doctor and team confirm they are able to handle a relationship. And, Ethel, they are chaperoned when together."

My shoulders lowered. I let out a deep breath as if I had been holding it for the entire time she was talking. I sat back in the chair. It felt like the air was being slowly released from a large balloon. And my body was the balloon.

I looked at my watch and began to gather my pocketbook. "Nurse Joanna, thank you. I feel better. And I would like to come back to see Dr. Redmond next week. Can I call on Monday to give y'all an update on my travel days?"

We both stood from the table. "Yes, of course. I will relay this information to Dr. Redmond and the team."

She smiled. It gave me comfort. I am not sure why I did this, but I did. I stepped over to her and gave her a hug, like I do when my family helps me out. She really did not participate in the hug, just patted my back gently. I guess that is how a nurse hugs.

Chapter 9 — March 15, 1946

Annie
Stressful Anticipation

ETHEL CALLED TO SAY SHE would be very late. "I missed the 12:35 train," she said, "so I am coming on the 4:35 one. I don't get to DC until bedtime. Go take a nap. You have got to wait up for me. We have so much to talk about. And it's not about you."

This time her call came from the train station. It was the shortest call on record. "Bottom line, Annie," she blurted out, "Caroline has turned into a girl courting a boy. Caroline is in love. Oh, heaven help us!"

None of that made sense at all. It was frankly not possible. Just when I was asking her to explain, I heard the train whistle in the background. "Gotta run, sister!" she said and hung up the telephone.

I was almost over being mad at Jon. He's been more attentive since the disaster of a day when we heard we were expecting twins. He explained how scared he was to be the father of four children. His exact quote was, "I really do worry about you giving birth to two humans. But when I heard 'twins,' my first thoughts were about money, the house, and my work. Not necessarily in that order. Selfish, I know, but dang it, Annie. I am the husband and father, and I didn't see a way to manage all that for my family."

Since that day, I have been listening more too. When I told Lelia about the twins, she was so excited for us all. "Oh, Miss Walsh, two more babies to love. Young'uns need lots of brothers and sisters. That way they learn to think about how to get along with all kinds of people."

I knew that was the truth.

As always with Lelia, she was ready to pitch in. "What do we need to do now? How long we got?"

I had calmed down after my first call with Ethel. She gave me a list of things to do. That always helped me get started on some new project. And this might be the biggest project I have ever done, except when I moved to Washington—all in one fell swoop. And look at the adventures I've had and what a good life that decision has given me.

In my notebook I made my list, a list for Jon, one for Lelia, and even one for Lisa. She was not yet five, but she really liked getting things done. If she wasn't busy, she would fuss with her brother. I never met Lisa's birth mother, but I imagine most of that side of Lisa was from her daddy. Keep me busy or I will make trouble.

With Ethel's visit as my deadline, I transformed Jon Jon's baby room for Ethel, so she would be happy to stay as long as she could and come back often. Lelia helped me move both children in one bedroom. The crib was packed up and stored in the attic, for now anyway. I bought another small bed so Lisa and Jon would have one just alike. His side of the room was painted sky blue and Lisa wanted her side yellow "like my room at the Hotel Sir Walter." I remembered it being like the yellow inside a pineapple. We could do that.

I never learned to sew as well as my sisters, but there are plenty of talented seamstresses in Washington. It turned out that Lelia's cousin Beula was one of them. She came and measured for everything we needed—curtains, bedspreads, and table covers, and she promised to get two quilts made before winter. "We can get you in line with the quilting ladies," Beula said proudly. I contributed some ideas about color, but she and Lelia picked out the perfect fabrics. What a treasure they are!

For Ethel's room we ordered all new furniture. I was able to find a store that had all we needed in stock and could deliver within a week. It was on display for customers so had bedding, lamps, a dresser and everything else we needed. Yippee! Check off the list!

Jon was coming home earlier from work these days. He would join me and admire what we had accomplished in the new spaces. Lelia and two of her family members were moving the new furniture around in Ethel's room this evening.

Jon doesn't often make suggestions on something like furniture but tonight he did. "Well, ladies, this will be a great place for Ethel. Something is missing though. There needs to be two comfortable chairs for this room. Ethel and Annie will spend hours in here talking away. Annie, go back to that furniture store and get two lady-sized chairs."

That idea unexpectedly hit me more deeply than he could have ever known. A powerful memory came to my mind. I stared at the room as if seeing exactly what was missing. I almost began to weep.

"Jon, you could never know how perfect that idea is. Have I told you about the chairs Momma made for us when we turned fifteen years old?" He shook his head.

I dropped on the bed and stretched out my arms to Lelia and my family to join me. "Come here, y'all, and let me tell you that story."

Lelia brought Lisa over, and we all gathered like our typical bedtime story tradition. I began unfolding the memory.

"When each of us girls turned fifteen, our mother gave us our thinking chair. She said when a girl grows to an age to begin planning her life, she needs a special chair. A chair that is comfortable for reading, writing, and thinking.

"I remember vividly when Dianne got hers. I was nearly eleven. It was the most beautiful chair I'd ever seen. It had wooden arms and legs made smooth by Jake and Tom, two of the workers on the farm. Momma used to say Jake and Tom could turn a tree branch into anything we needed and given the time, they also could make it a thing of beauty. I learned pretty quickly that they also made toys from stumps and doll baby beds out of broken pieces of something. Most years at Christmas, Jake and Tom made wooden toys, stick horses, and small rockers for children. They sold them at the general store in town, so they could buy some fine Christmas presents for their wives and families.

"It wasn't until Ethel got her special chair that I understood the significance of this gift. Momma let me 'help' Jake and Tom decide on the shape of Ethel's chair. I told them Ethel would want one with big fabric arms and a big enough seat for me to sit with her. Momma and I went to town to pick out the fabric. Ethel got to tell us what color she wanted, but the rest was to be a surprise. Ethel chose the color of watermelon. She said that was the sweetest food on a hot summer day.

"The base was a solid construction by Jake and Tom. Momma packed lamb's wool or horse hair around the frame and then tightly covered it with a fabric that seem to be exactly right for each of us. I remember the men who made these chairs seem to know when our fifteenth birthday was approaching. They would begin collecting the best wood, decorative nails, and supplies for their "secret" project for one of us girls. We would all get just as excited. My chair was green, as dark as a Christmas tree."

It felt good telling this story and remembering all of us at home. I grabbed Jon's hand and said, "Jon, getting two lady chairs is a great idea, but I don't want to buy them pre-made. I have the one Momma made for me, but it needs new fabric. Lelia, you seem to have talents of all kind in your family. Do you know someone who could make another chair to match? I want them to be the same shape and fabric, just different colors."

Lelia smiled big. "You should see Uncle Samuel's wood work. He can make anything out of any wood. I'll ask him. Also, Beula is teaching me how to do upholstery. We can do that together. I would be so glad to help make 'em fine for you and your sister."

"Perfect," I replied as Jon gave a big smile of approval.

Once we found out we were expecting, Jon decided we should hire a housekeeper and cook. At first, I thought it seemed senseless, but now that we are expecting two more children, I agreed that it was a smart idea. Elaine Jefferson, the lovely woman who wanted to "do keeping house and filling your bellies," began right away. Thank goodness she and Lelia hit it off. Because if she was not a good fit with Lelia, Elaine could not stay. Lelia was as close to family as anyone ever came outside of my sisters, our children and my husband. And she was essential to me being able to make it through what was to come.

At seven sharp Jon, the children, and I sat down for dinner that Elaine prepared. I was tired but excited. Very soon Ethel would be here. I kept myself from calling her before she arrived, so I could show her instead of tell her how much I was getting done. As we ate, I asked Jon about the fears he had about the babies—the house, work, and money.

"Annie, I have not made as much progress as you

have toward being ready for the twins, but I am not worried or scared. Whatever is needed will work out. One piece of good news is about my pay. When I told the general about my expanding family, he gave me a raise in pay. He said a man with a proper family needed a big salary. He also is arranging for my pension to be increased. He said, 'It is not only clothes and food these new children will need. They will need to go to college.'"

I was delighted. One thing is for sure. I will need more household money to manage this family of six! This night our dinner together seemed like old times. We talked about the future and how fortunate we were. I felt like we really could make this work. It might have been the scrumptious food or Jon being more relaxed, but I was feeling more content than I had in a long time. And my sister was on the way!

~~~

The house was quiet. Everyone had gone to bed. Lelia and Elaine left hours ago. I was writing in my diary not only about what was happening with the two babies in me but how I was nesting to prepare for their arrival. The items on the lists were getting checked off. When items I listed for others were not, I added them to my list. Now I had the time. In a few months, there would be no time to do what I wanted.

I heard a car door shut and then a knock at the door downstairs. I jumped up and dashed like a five-year-old girl running downstairs to see what Santa brought. I opened the door and there she was. My sister. My best friend.

"Hot diggity dog, Ethel. You are here! I have been ready and waiting for hours!"

She shifted the misery. "I called and told you I'd be late. And you've not been the one sitting for hours in a train car packed with rude people. What's going on in town? Why are there so many people coming here at once?"

Laughing, I reminded her, "Ethel, this is a big city. There are hordes of people coming and going all the time. Saturday is tourist travel day. They are coming to see spring in their nation's capital. I hope the cherry blossoms burst while you are here. It's like nothing you've ever seen. Give me your bag. I have coffee brewing for us. And we have so much to talk about."

As she began climbing the stairs, Ethel seemed stressed out. "You're right about having a lot to talk about. You have no idea! But I need the washroom first and to get out of these uncomfortable train clothes. I don't know why we dress up to ride a train with strangers anyway."

I was giddy about showing her the new room. I told her it was hers for as long and as many times as I could have her. She got tearful when I told her about the chairs that were being made ready for us. "I miss Momma all the time," she said as her eyes filled with water.

"Me too, especially now," I replied.

Before getting us started on a long night of conversation, I suggested, "Put on your night clothes and join me in the living room. We'll have some canapés and whatever you want to drink."

Ethel raised her eyebrows and smiled, "Can a peas?

I just want some snacks and a fine cocktail. Maybe that Sidecar you introduced me to at the Hotel Sir Walter. That was lip-smacking powerful stuff."

My sister and I talked, debated, and shared all that had happened in both of our lives. I now understood what happened with the Caroline visit and why she was frightened. It was a fear for different reasons than I understood earlier. I disagreed with her that Caroline having a boyfriend would be so terrible. "Having a man's love can be the best thing for Caroline. Look what is has done for us, Ethel!"

We discussed motherhood, no matter how it comes to you. I presented my side of the story. "Caroline has always loved children. If she gets pregnant, and Joe is a good man, he and the staff at Dix Hill will make sure she is a responsible mother. And of course, she has us to keep a check on her. Just like you are making sure I do this twins thing well."

Ethel seemed open to another perspective, but she knew this story all too well. "When babies come, there is nothing more important than being a good mother. And it's not easy. Remember—men cannot be relied on."

Okay, I was ready for this. We have had this discussion many times. Now it was time to end this blame. "Ethel, you are wrong. If you are talking about Frank, you have to remember that you also did not work on keeping that relationship together. You could have gone to Virginia with him. You could have let Marie know her daddy from the beginning. You are right that Frank selfishly did what his parents demanded of him—he left you and Marie behind. He told you time and time again how sorry he was and how his decision had been wrong. All he could think about was being able to financially support his family."

Sometime during the evening, Ethel had switched over to spicing up her coffee with a little whiskey which probably explained what happened next. Ethel erupted into a crying jag. "I knew you always blamed me for not marrying Frank. You thought he was handsome and figured that made him a good man. But a good man does not choose his parents over the 'love of his life'! He left me with a baby. We were nearly children ourselves. I could not forgive that! And I am not to blame!" Ethel was shaking all over.

Hoping to slow the torrent of words and anger, I said calmly, "Ethel, I'm sorry. I can't know how you felt or still feel. But what I do know is that Frank has spent most of his life trying to get you to forgive him. How long will you carry that? It has been nearly twenty years. Your heart will mend. The blame will be gone when you can forgive him. Listen to your own words and apply them to Caroline—a good man does not choose his parents over the 'love of his life.' By standing in the way of Caroline's happiness, you are filling the role that the Pollards did in keeping Frank away from you. We can't repeat that in this family."

Ethel's face turned grey. She plopped down on the sofa and cried. She cried as hard as I have seen in a long time. Her body shook, and she let out an agonized wail. It was as if something in her soul had cracked. I sat next to her and grabbed her shoulders. I worked to breathe easily and calmly. Stroking her hair, I said, "Breathe, big sister. Breathe. Let it loose. Let it out."

I am not sure how long we sat like that, but we woke holding each other's hand. I remembered doing that as a child. Either it was Ethel, Dianne, Caroline, Momma, or all of us together. But when times were tough, we slept holding hands in the same bed. Every time, the morning sun would rise, and we would work through the problems together.

It was amazing we did not wake Jon and the children. They did not join us until Ethel and I were having breakfast and writing our ideas and plans on several sheets of paper.

Jon entered the room carrying JJ with Lisa trailing behind. "Good morning, ladies. Looks like you are solving the problems of the world."

CHAPTER 10 — JUNE 1946

Ethel
Angels All Around

CAROLINE AND I HAD a productive visit on my return from Annie's house in March. Spending time with Annie helped me heal a very old wound. I have never given Annie enough credit on the wise-one scale. She was always the younger sister. My attitude with Caroline shifted even before I met with her doctor and care team. I now knew I couldn't stand in the way of her happiness. I just needed to pay close attention so I could see if the path was leading wrong for her.

I also was able to meet Joseph (Joe) Kirkpatrick while there. Although I wanted to dislike him, he was quite the gentleman. It was obvious he cared for Caroline. He frequently praised her to me as if I didn't know my sister. He said things like, "Caroline is so smart. She knows a lot about gardening. Did you know she is teaching herself to play the guitar?" He held the door for her and for me. He was perceptive of her and rushed to get things for her before she asked.

It was evident that she was in "puppy love" with him. She giggled like a school girl when he was around. She used every chance to brush up against him when walking and touched his arm or shoulder when he spoke about her.

I needed to know more about him from Dr. Redmond. Nurse Joanna had been right. Dr. Redmond did know about the relationship that was building between Joe and Caroline. He couldn't tell me everything about this young (five years younger than Caroline) man, but he told me as much as he thought would help me trust Caroline's choice.

"Mrs. Martin, I have asked Joe's permission to share some things about his life. He says he will be glad to meet and answer questions you might have. Joe grew up in eastern North Carolina. He was the oldest of three siblings—two boys and one girl. Like most men of the last generation, his father served in the first World War and was about to re-enlist after the attack on Pearl Harbor. But his two sons begged him to stay home this time and said they would go. The younger son, Paul, fought in France but was sent home in 1944 after being severely injured. He did not survive his wounds. Joe took it really hard, as anyone would. Since Joe had been trained in machine mechanics before joining the army, he had been sent to a newly built Army base on the coast of North Carolina. The work that they were doing on the island out from Camp Davis was top secret. All the men were isolated from family. Joe will tell you that without family, he could not deal with the demons that were ruling his mind.

He says that the angels of those who have passed on have tremendous power over his actions. Ethel, he is eager to tell all of us that the trick is making sure the angels win and the demons lose."

I had listened closely to understand how any of this related to Caroline. The information about family, angels, and demons made it crystal clear. I now cared differently for this man. I was sure Caroline felt the importance of family, which she holds dear, as the bond of this relationship.

Those days back in March when I was at Annie's in "my room" seemed like a long time ago. Now I am back. The babies are getting ready to greet the world. Annie is having some early distress. As soon as I got the call, I drove to the train station in Raleigh and jumped on the earliest train to DC. This time I was not be able to visit Caroline. For now, Annie and the future Nash-Walsh children demanded my attention.

Sure enough, when I arrived, Annie was already in distress. In fact, she had left home to go to the hospital.

The new woman at Annie's house, Elaine (she pronounces it Eee lane), told me about Annie's morning. "Miss Martin, Miss Walsh didn't sleep much. When I arrived at seven this morning, Mr. Walsh was a mess. He was pacing around in his sleeping clothes giving me a play-by-play of Miss Walsh's condition. He was like a rat in a roomful of cats. Much of what he said didn't make sense. He was going on about Annie not being able to have these babies and that she could die.

"I rushed back to see Miss Walsh and knew by the looks of her she was ready to get those babies out.

Her water had come, and the color of it was not right. I called the doctor and said, 'Miss Walsh needs to have these babies. Is she gonna have them here or in your hospital?' He said to have Mr. Walsh bring her in. But I knew that wasn't gonna happen. Mr. Walsh needed a doctor of his own. I told the doctor he needed to send an ambulance, that Mr. Walsh was busy having his own conniption. So that's what they did.

"Before Miss Walsh was put into the ambulance, she was giving orders. 'Elaine, call Lelia and get her here to help you with the children. Call my sister Ethel and tell her I need her. Those numbers are by the phone.

"Miss Martin, that was a few hours ago. I don't think she has had those babies yet or she would have ordered Mr. Walsh to call. Oh, thank the Lord you are here!"

Elaine stepped outside and summoned the driver. I jumped in the car almost forgetting how uppity I looked. It's a far cry from the first Nash baby that was brought into this world. Dianne and I rode to town in the wagon pulled by our mule, Sadie. And it was on the way that we realized my baby was coming and didn't want to wait until the shopping at the General Store was finished. I busted the dam right on the wagon that day. I don't remember much of the details after that, but Dianne loved to tell the story about me falling off the wagon (no, not the way some people do) and getting covered in dirt and mud. It was fitting that I was a mess when Marie was arriving. Life is kind of a mess. Marie got used to it from the beginning.

I arrived at the hospital lickety-split, rushed in the

front door and demanded to know about my sister. "Where is Annie Nash Walsh? I am her sister and ready to help bring her babies here!" Then I noticed there were about ten people in the waiting room. Evidently, we are not the only ones having a baby this morning.

"Ethel, thank goodness you are here. I am worried sick!" There stood Jon, the high-ranking officer in the War Department disheveled, wet from sweat, with wild looking eyes. "They won't let me back there. I have been here hours drinking coffee by the gallon and wishing it was something stronger."

"Jon, you look like you should cut down on the coffee. Nothing stronger. Have you eaten? Go find some breakfast, and I will go in and see what is going on." I said, although not really sure, "She will be fine."

This tall, brave man, who rarely shows emotion leaned down and wrapped his arms around me. "She has got to be alright. I can't lose another love of my life."

If this man really had tears, they would be flooding out.

"I know, Jon. Get some food in your belly, and I will see what is happening with our Annie and those babies." I turned and walked toward the door that was labeled DELIVERY.

I must have looked like someone to reckon with, or at least someone who was supposed to do this, because no one stopped me from going through that door. The hallway ahead of me had three doors on each side. There was a lot of screaming going on. I figured there must be several babies trying to come into this world right now. I wondered how I would find Annie. It would be bad manners to just go in everyone's room searching for my sister. For a minute I stood quiet at the front of the hallway, then I heard her. It was a blood-curdling scream. Not the kind of cry I had ever heard from my sister. It was the kind of scream women make when trying to push out a way-too-big baby from her body. But that scream was from my sister. I followed the sound, calling to her, "Annie, I'm coming!"

That got more attention than I wanted. A woman dressed in a nurse uniform stepped in front of me and commanded, "Excuse me, you can't be back here!"

Another person grabbed my arm. Oh no, that is not going to happen! I called out for Annie again. Then she hollered back. "Ethel, oh Ethel. I am in here. Please help me!" The nurse looked at me and said, "If you are not a medical expert, you cannot be back here."

Clever that I was, I used my bossy tone and lied. "I am a medical expert! I have birthed many babies on my own. And that is my sister. She will have my medical expertise by her bed as the doctor delivers those babies. Believe me, you and the doctor will be glad you let me in there. If something happens to the general's wife or his children there will be hell to pay."

Okay, Jon is not a general. Frankly, I don't know what he is, but it worked. I was not sure if it was my convincing lecture or the doctor poking his head out of the room yelling to the baby security, "Let her come in. I could use her help in calming the patient." I like to think it was my talent of persuasion.

I entered the room and saw nothing except Annie thrashing in pain on a bed covered in blood. It looked like she had already had the babies. I grabbed the hand that had a tight grip on the bedsheet. "I'm here, baby girl. I am here. Where are the babies?"

Then Annie sank back to the bed and her body calmed. "They won't come out, Ethel. They can't get out!"

I shifted my gaze to the doctor. It was a look of fear and anger. I knew better than to make him mad, but I needed to know some things.

"How long has she been in labor?"

"Six hours of mild contractions. The last couple of hours of intermittently intense pains. Her body is working hard to get those babies positioned. It could be anytime now."

I put my hands on Annie's swollen belly and began to massage. I saw Momma do that once when she was helping a neighbor deliver a really big baby. There was a lot of moving going on inside. I began to rub harder, deeper. Then I felt a something like a volcano beginning to erupt. Another inhuman scream shot out of Annie's mouth. I went back to holding her hands. I leaned down toward Annie's head and began humming "America the Beautiful." After the screaming and pain subsided, she looked at me and began to giggle. "Let's sing it, Annie. Let's sing a most beautiful song." And we did. We sang the entire first verse before the pain began again.

During the pain screams, two nurses in the room joined in. All of us but the doctor were singing loudly but not in unison because Annie had to scream between words. Oh well, it was working.

Dr. what's-his-name spoke above the choir, "Here comes one of babies, Annie. Here it comes!" Then looking over at me, he added, "Sister, don't stop singing. Sing so these babies can join in!"

I moved down to see the baby. It was tiny. And so still. The nurse must have noticed the worry on my face. She took the baby and gave it a swift slap on the bottom. Then another. As we were all staring at the baby, a small but fierce wail come out of that tiny child. To myself I said a prayer I often do, "Thank you, Momma." I went back to the head of the bed and whispered to Annie, "The angel of Momma brought you a baby girl. Another Nash girl."

As the nurse was cleaning that blessing of a baby, Annie was crying softly with her hands outstretched. "Bring her to me. I must see her. I must hear her breathing."

The swaddled miracle was laid on Annie's chest, and I leaned in close. I needed to hear it too. Their breathing must be in sync just like when Marie was born. I knew back then we would all be okay when my breath, Marie's breath, and my momma's breath moved into a rhythmic bond.

Annie looked at me whispering, "There it is. Ethel, do you hear it?"

"Yes, dear sister. I hear it. And I know Momma does too."

I don't know how long it was, but it was enough to be thankful for the peace. Then the volcano began to rumble again. The doctor said, "Get ready and let's bring out this other child. It's time for the next one to get into position."

The nurse took our baby and said, "She will be waiting for you in the baby room. I will go let your husband know he has a healthy girl."

Annie was exhausted. I was worried she could not do it again. I needed to make sure I believed she could. "Round number two, Annie girl! Just one more baby into our family and then you can rest. You can do this!"

Annie summoned the strength. She didn't have much choice because the pain began and her belly began squeezing and releasing, squeezing and releasing. For what seemed like forever, this went on with no calm between contractions. Annie's body looked like it was not hers. It was doing the delivery without her. Annie looked frail. Her voice was faint. "I can't. I can't do anymore."

I stood to look at the doctor. He read my mind. Annie needed reassurance. "Annie, you are almost there. I see that baby's head. You are going to need to push a little more so I can help you. You give me one more really hard push, and I will bring the baby out."

I put my arms behind her back and slid behind her on the bed. I pulled her body to nearly a sitting position and gathered my fragile sister in my arms, "Push, Annie, push!"

She mustered the strength and cried out nearly as loud as in the beginning. I yelled, "Come on, angel Momma. Help our Annie!"

Then she collapsed. Her eyes closed; her body

motionless. I gently laid her back on the bed. I could not hear her breathing.

Evidently it had been enough. The doctor moved from the bottom of the bed to the top. He was frantically wiping his hands and beckoning her back to us. "Annie, you did it. You have two babies. This one is a boy. Stay with us, Annie. There is a little more work to do, so I need you here with us. Then you can rest."

She wasn't responding. I started shaking her. "Annie, get back in this room! You have more chores to do. You can sleep, but don't leave us. Do you hear me, Annie? You must be here, in this room. Breathe, breathe slow, but breathe. Let me hear that heartbeat, Annie. Just show us you are here!"

The nurse who had her stethoscope on Annie's chest was concentrating only on what was happening in her ears. I bent down to Annie's face and started singing to the tune of "America the Beautiful" again, but this time it was only the second verse with words for Annie.

Oh Annie girl, oh Annie girl,
God shed his grace on thee.
And crown your good with familyhood
From Lisa to baby three.

Then all I could do is cry softly in her ear. "Stay with me, Annie. Stay with all of us. We need you."

The nurse spoke, "There is a heartbeat. It's weak, but it is there." Now the doctor moved his stethoscope from the heart to the lungs and back again. "Yes, and her breathing is slow but steady. She is coming back."

I had forgotten there was another baby. I had not heard a peep from it. Two nurses were working on the other side of the room behind a curtain.

The questions came quickly as I moved toward the curtain. "Is the baby okay. What is it? A boy or girl? I don't hear it." A man I did not recognize stretched out his arm and said, "Please stay there so we can work with the boy. I am a pediatric doctor, and we need to focus on him."

I plopped on a chair by Annie. As tears slid down my face I murmured, "A boy. Annie, you brought us a girl and a boy." I looked upward and said, "Momma, she did two at once."

CHAPTER 11

Happy/Sad Nash Round-Robin Letters

Saturday, January 4, 1947

Dear Family, and especially Dear Annie.

Since this will be the first page you read upon opening these letters, I want you to know how HAPPY SAD I am every day for you and the Walsh family. It has been a half a year since you were in the hospital having the babies. I am so glad we came to see you before I went back to school. Little Dianne is so precious. She squeezes so good and smells divine! And you looked beautiful. Less smile on your face, but so much love in your heart. Thank you for letting me see you and talk a long time about me. Auntie Annie, I love you to the moon and back!

Another year has passed and a chance for happiness arrives with the new year. Christmas wasn't the same this year. It was quiet with just the four of us on Christmas Eve and Christmas day. My holiday memories are centered around you all. I don't remember a year when no one came here or when we stayed home. I am still here in Burlington, bored. If it wasn't for Suzy, I'd go nuts. Of course, neither Suzy nor I will tell Momma that. If we did, out would come the DO IT list. Suzy is super good at looking busy, mostly by staying out of sight and changing her location occasionally. Oops, I just spilled the beans. Sorry, Suzy. Momma, I was just kidding. Suzy is always very, very busy.

There is good news buzzing around here, but I'll let Momma tell you in her letter. And Suzy, don't forget to tell everyone about your new career. Oh, the suspense of it all!

My life is as expected—studying, listening to the radio, playing records, going out to dances, and visiting Aunt Caroline as often as I can get away. And yes, I am still seeing Al. I guess you can say we are an item. I even think he may be <u>the one</u>. He is nice to me. We have a lot in common. He is a hard worker. Although he lives and works in Raleigh, he goes to the family farm to help with planting and harvest. He served in the Army, but not in battle. I am fine with that. One thing I worry about is he likes to be in charge. Most of the time I let him choose what we are going to do and where we are going. If it doesn't matter, why not? Al sets goals for himself, which for now include me.

And he recently told me it also included a wife and lots of children. I like the idea of someday having a husband but am not sure about lots of children.

Momma, Suzy, and N-D-L met Al when they came to bring my stuff home for Christmas. That was N-D-L's idea. He said before they came that I should arrange for "this fella to put on a nice shirt, tuck it in, and come meet your family. I need to know who his people are."

I can see all of you across these miles breathing in and raising your eyebrows because that is exactly what I did when he said that. Heck, I didn't even know who his people are. I guess that is one thing I need to know if we really are in this for the long term.

You have heard me talk about Izzy. She's my roommate at State. She is super smart but doesn't care much about studying. She doesn't have to. Izzy just shows up to class and she makes an A. I, on the other hand, have to study like crazy and go to class. Izzy calls me an old fuddy-duddy because I don't go to the fraternity house parties. At the beginning of this semester, she told me I have to go to these things. She says coming to State College is not about getting an education. It's about getting a husband.

This was the first time we argued about anything. I told her that was nuts. I said, "Are you kidding me, Izzy? Do you really think women should go to college to find a man?" I about flipped my lid. That makes women submissive to men. If we have to work hard to get a man, then women become someone a particular man wants instead of who she wants to be!

Izzy answered me back real quick. "Hold on, Marie," she said, "This is a numbers game. Where else will we find a man with a career and money? Men with a degree in engineering make good money. You and I are in a group of fewer than sixty women on this campus with 5,000 men. How on earth are we going to know which man we want to marry? These house parties slim down the odds while we have a blast!"

I got mad as a hornet. I said, "Dang it all, Izzy, I want my own degree. I want to make my own career. I don't need a man for that! And neither do you. You are too smart to let a man lead you around by the collar!"

"At least it will be a diamond collar!" Izzy yelled and stomped out the door.

As y'all can imagine, Izzy and I are no longer friends. We just pass each other in the hallway. Frankly, Izzy's attitude is what is wrong today. We have the right to vote, but few women do. Did you know there are only 11 women who have been elected to Congress? That means 235 men are deciding laws about child labor and mental health resources. What happens to all the families whose men have come home from the war sick or disabled? They fought for our country, but they can't feed their family. And most important to me and my nieces, men are deciding whether women can work in any job she is qualified for. I may be able to earn a degree, but most likely I can only get a job as a teacher, nurse, secretary – or just a wife.

YIKES! I just flipped my lid on this paper. Sorry, guys and gals. I just couldn't stop. So, I better end this letter. You know I love y'all, no matter what job you do, right?

Shut my mouth.
Marie

Monday January 6, 1947

Hello.

To all my wonderful family who have found really good men and those who don't need them, are you still reading? Or did you just put these letters down out of anger or are laughing? Marie, what would we do without your preaching? You may have your sights on the wrong career. You should be a preacher or maybe go into politics. I'll support you in anything you want. I'm afraid not to. TEE HEE

As you all know, I decided not to go to college. I can't imagine how we can afford that anyway. Dad/Larry and Momma are teaching me the biz. The world of having something of my own and making a living out of it. Once I told them I did not want to follow in Marie's footsteps, Momma said, "Make a plan then, girlie. What will you do with yourself the rest of your life?"

I bought a typewriter with my Christmas money. Thank y'all for helping me get started. That is why my letter is no longer in longhand. I enjoy typing and am learning to get faster at it.

I took a job at the textile plant here in Burlington, but that is not my career. It is just a way to save money for the next move.

I have done some research. It costs about $6,000 to buy a new home. A new car costs over $1,000. Of course, I will not be buying anything new. Something used with some character is all I need. This job is a line worker at the textile factory. It's the best thing for now at $1.05 an hour. Dad and Momma said I can live here and save rent on a place. At least for now. That could fit right into my plan. I really appreciate it, Momma and Dad!

I am off at the factory on Sunday because they say it is God's day, so I help with the laundromat and ice cream shop on these days. Momma says my wages are three straight meals a day.

The only thing I do for fun is read. Right now, I am reading <u>The Adventures of Tom Sawyer</u>. Next, I am moving on to any other Mark Twain books. Annie, with the money you sent me for Christmas you said to put aside some for only myself to have fun, not for the plan. I will do that. I am going to see the Tom Sawyer movie as soon as it comes to a theater nearby. And I also bought some more books. Thank you!

I am thinking of y'all every day. Things seem dreary right now. It is cold, the sky is gray, and our hearts are heavy. Sadness hit us hard this past year. We are getting by, but it is tricky. You often say the Nash girls' strength comes from each other. Yet we are far apart. I am sad for my aunties and need hugs from my cousins. Please let's make sure we see each other often so we can sing, dance, and laugh together. That will soften our tears.

Love,

Suzy

Saturday, January 11, 1947

Hello People!

Thanks, Suzy, for sending this to me. I guess Ethel was out and about and couldn't get her letter done before sending. That works for me but not sure who to send to next. Ethel, I think I will send back to you so Annie will have all our thoughts in one package.

Annie. Dear, dear Annie. My heart is broken because I did not come to see you after the birth of the babies. Ethel told me that she will figure out how to bring me to Washington in the spring.

I wanted to meet Thomas. I wanted to hold his hand and kiss off all the sugar on his neck. I hope the few days he was with us, you or someone got that sugar.

Ethel told me as much as I could handle about how brave and strong you were when bringing Dianne and Thomas into this world. She said that Thomas tried as hard as he could, but breathing air outside his momma was too hard for him. I believe, our momma and papa needed him. God needs good angels all the time, and Momma wanted him in her lap and Papa needed to have one of our little boys. I am mad at God for taking him. I cried for days after I heard. Dr. Redmond and the nurses all knew what was going on, thanks to Marie. They gave me extra time to talk about it, and we tried a new medicine and therapy. They were afraid I would not pull out of the depression. I stopped going to the chapel here. I could not go and praise God when he took Thomas.

The Christmas holy service was on Sunday before Christmas. I did not go. Joe tried to convince me it might help me understand. He thought maybe I would get a sign from God through the pastor. Y'all know when I am well enough to do it, I go to the chapel service every week. On that Sunday before Christmas, I sat with Joe at breakfast in my house kitchen. Everyone else had gone to church. He doesn't usually talk about his faith, but this day he did.

Holding my hand and watching me, Joe told me his story in a different way than I'd heard before. "Caroline, you know I am damaged goods. The war really screwed with my head. Not from what I saw, but because I did not have the chance to save my brother or fight in his place. The last time I saw my brother was when we both left basic training at Camp Bragg.

"Caroline, God did not ask my opinion about who went where. He did not show me why I was chosen to live. All I could think about was why I was being punished. I threw myself into my work during the day and drank heavily at night. That seemed to ease the pain. The job I was doing made it easy to pull away from people—to do what I wanted. Non-stop I was battering my body by working like a dog for the Army and the endless drinking and doping. If someone looked crossways at me or said something I didn't like, I would beat them up. As you know, I spent a lot of time in jail and hospitals. That life was serving a purpose. I no longer felt anything. It made it easier to forget what my brother's face must have looked like after it was blown apart."

I needed him to stop talking, so I said, "Joe, why are you telling me this? That is not who you are now. How can reliving it help you or me?"

Joe moved closer to me and said something

I needed to hear. "Caroline, you can't pull away from God. You are angry for Annie. And you're scared. Frankly, things like this frighten me too. You and I are different from others. We have been to the depths of loneliness and hopelessness. And it is hard to pull out of that without help. I cannot and do not want you to go there again. Annie is broken-hearted. The family has lost the most precious thing possible—a life. With the help of the doctors and staff here, I have learned I can't fix what happened to my brother. It is in the past. All I can do is move on to be the best person I can. To live a life that is deserving of having a brother until he was 17. To be worthy of this life. I need God so I can remember that. And I need you with me to see there is happiness in my future."

The Christmas service was over by the time we walked to the chapel. I asked Joe to let me go in by myself. He kissed my cheek and stepped away. "I'll be right here when you come out."

I went in the chapel which was smelling of pine boughs, cinnamon, and bread. It was familiar. Not only from what it smells like every Christmas, but what home was like during the winter. Annie, it brought me so close to you that I could almost feel you. You were praying with me saying the words our church preacher said every Sunday. As a child, I used to call it the Our Father prayer. I prayed so hard. I cried and I prayed. Then I saw Momma. She was that angel we always imagined. She sat beside us both. She said, "I have Thomas. He is so lovely and in no pain. He looks like Jon, but he has the determination of you, Annie. Your papa, me, and Thomas want you to live a good life. We will watch over you while you heal from this."

The tears stopped. I knew Momma was right and Joe too. We have work to do. I have to be well enough to live the life I want to, not in this place. And you, Annie, have to be a mother to Lisa, JJ, and Dianne, just as you are meant to be. Thomas will always be the scar in your heart. And your heart will beat strongly that way.

I need to stop. I will finish this letter later.

Monday, January 13, 1947

I just re-read what I wrote, and I thought about ripping it up. It is too sad. And I worry you might think the ghost thing with Annie and Momma is my crazies rearing up. But I decided to keep it.

I am sure you all talked about me when you were in DC with Annie and the babies. Other than what I already said, I am gonna tell you what is going on with me.

Y'all know I am head over heels smitten with Joe Kirkpatrick. We have such fun together. We talk about everything. Dr. Mark says I am benefiting from a friend like Joe. Dr. Mark has no idea how I am benefiting. Tee hee.

Since Christmas is over and things are looking up, I decided to keep a diary. Joe bought me a note-book and pens in various colors to get started. It was way too horrible to write things down earlier in my life. Now writing about my moods, healing, and a TO DO list feels right.

I thought you would like to see my TO DO list. But, Ethel, this does not give you permission to nag me about getting the list checked off.

Caroline's TA DA TO DO LIST — January 1947

Everyday
- Get exercise every day. Write down what I did today.
- Eat healthy things. Write them here.
- Do my chores in the house. Which did I do?
- Be thankful for Joe and everyone who helps me.
- Take my medicine every kind at the right time.

This Week
- Write thank you notes for Christmas gifts
- Practice playing the guitar. Learn a new song.
- Finish and send the Nash Round-Robin Letter
- Write in my diary about how I feel — good and bad

This Month
- Follow doctor's orders
- Nag Ethel about taking me to Washington, DC!
- Read two new books.

See, y'all – I am doing better.

Happy New Year to my family,
Caroline

Sunday, January 19, 1947

Dear Nash Girls and the men who care about them,

These letters tell me a lot more about y'all! Even though we call each other on the telephone, we really don't talk about what you write in these letters.

WOW – Caroline, you blew me away. You opened a side of you in your letter I had not heard since our childhood. Thank you. We all needed that.

Suzy, you think I know everything about what's going on with you, but every time you write these letters, I learn something new. Doing research on the cost of a car and a house and setting a plan. Yippee, girl!!

Marie, I'm glad you are holding your own with Izzy. You and she can be friends but stand tall in being who you think you should be. Follow your own lead. I'm proud of you, baby girl – in so many ways.

Annie, don't you just swell up from all the love on these pages? I do. You know how I feel about what has happened to you. It is sad, horrible, and unfair. As I read these letters, I remember how many times the Nash family has needed to bounce back from pain and misery. And we do. So will you, my sweet sister. I am thankful that you and I got to spend many days and weeks together around all this. It was the happy part of our sad.

Larry really pulled the load around here in 1946, and it was not only in the truck. He ran the business by himself. And Suzy is his trusted assistant in pulling that load. He stopped hauling stuff for the truck driving company when I went to stay with Annie. Before leaving, I did a crash course with him on keeping up the books, so we got the bills paid on time. It turns out both the ice cream store and the laundromat had a really good year. Not sure how that happened, but I don't want to jinx it. When I asked how he did it, he explained, "Work hard, never say no to a customer, cut costs, and charge more. When the customer is happy, they will pay more. Simple as that."

Simple as that, hmm . . . I was jealous that I hadn't done it. But I stayed out of it. I told myself when business is good, don't get in the way.

In the fall after we closed the ice cream business for the year, Larry and I celebrated as we always do, eating all the leftover ice cream as if it won't keep. This year we made extra and invited the neighbors over to finish it off. Larry set up the picnic tables in the back lot. We decorated the tables with red checkered table cloths, pumpkins, and arrangements of fall mums that grew everywhere. Larry invited all our customers. Many of the people that came by I did not know. He talked to each and every one while Suzy and I served them. I was a little afraid we would run out of ice cream.

When it was all over and we had cleaned up, I grabbed my man and said, "Holy moly, so many people! You are a real find, Mr. Martin. I am exhausted, but I betcha these people will be customers for life!"

Suzy had a lot of fun with the customers. After everyone left, she said, "If we just get one more dollar out of everyone one of those people, and they tell one more person, we are in the money! The Kooler is a big business now!"

Larry was as happy as Suzy and I were. He said, "I had the best time meeting these folks. Thanks for letting me play maître d'." He gave me a squeeze, planted a big kiss on my cheek, and reminded me of a promise I made years ago. "Now am I a full partner in the company?"

"Yessiree!"

The next day I added his name to the legal papers and the tax forms. The Kooler is officially owned by the Martins.

Here is the news that Marie let out of the bag. We might be moving! Lock, stock, and barrel.

It probably won't happen until next year. Marie and Suzy know this, but I told them to keep it under their hats until we can work out the details. Caroline, after meeting Joe and him telling us about his work at Camp Davis and on the island of Topsail, Larry went to check it out. There are civilians living on the island, but not many. The few businesses they operate serve the military. Larry got a lot of information out of them. He is such a chatty man.

They say that Camp Davis is closing down. The operation on the island needs more space, so they are moving that secret mission somewhere else. Larry thinks the land will be sold really cheap. There is electric and water piped in and the roads were all built by the government. The locals say they won't want to take all that down. They will just move out leaving it behind.

We know this is all rumor right now, and we will keep looking for official information. It might be a risky adventure, but it could be the bargain of a lifetime! Getting in early, before the prices are too high, on an island with great fishing and stunning beaches is a great idea. How about The Kooler at Topsail Island with ice cream galore and washing all the clothes?! We would be living at the beach. Y'all could visit the "re-sort" anytime!

I am hoping to see you all soon. When winter moves away, I am getting in the car and coming to see every one of you. Keep the light on!

Your big business owner sister,

(the business is big, not your sister)

Ethel

Wednesday, January 22, 1947

Dearest Ethel, Larry, Caroline (and Joe), Marie (and Al), Suzy, and my beloved Jon,

I wanted to put all the names in just in case we someday forget who was around on this date. It took this letter a long time to get to me. We need to add a rule about not holding the letter too long. It is such a treasure to read. It made today a good day.

I love you all for saying such wonderful things. As Momma would say, last year was a hard row to hoe. I am healing both physically and mentally. I spend a lot of time with the children to make sure I remember what gifts I have.

Lelia and Elaine have helped me so much. It is like they know what this might be like. One day a few weeks ago before they were to leave for the evening, I was having a cup of tea in the kitchen. I was listening to the radio and singing along. Sweet Dianne was in my arms. She had finished nursing and showed that contented face. I felt a rush of warmth around me like I was in a protective bubble. I looked up to see both Elaine and Lelia watching me. They grabbed each other's hands and smiled. I stopped singing and looked at them. Elaine said, "Miss Walsh, do you know what is happening right now? You are being surrounded by the white light of love and protection."

Lelia walked to me and bent down on her knees. She looked up at me and spoke as if amazed, "I seen it too. I heard tell of it but ain't never seen it. Oh Lord, thank you for answering our prayers. Your heart is healing. I see it. Can you feel it, Miss Annie?"

It was strange but true. I felt something. It was someone's hand on my shoulder. It felt like positivity radiating around me. When we were children at church, the preacher used to talk about the hand of God. I don't think it was that. It was our momma's hand covering Dianne's hand, covering Thomas's small hand. I said to Lelia, "I feel love and caring. I feel strength from that. I feel happiness without guilt."

Those two wonderful women came near to

envelope me and Dianne in their arms. That caress was powerful. You were all in it with me. I cried as hard as I have ever cried. Elaine spoke in a soothing voice, "Cry, dear woman. Cry until you can't anymore. You are protected."

Lelia joined in, "Let it out, Miss Annie. The hurt in your heart is pourin' out. You will be healed. Amen."

Nash women, that was such an amazing experience. I can't describe it adequately, but I know I was changed in that moment. Thomas will never leave my heart. Even though he was ours for a brief time on earth, he will forever be a part of me. His short life will guide me for the rest of mine. Please do not worry about me. I will live a good and happy life because of the gift of Thomas, Dianne, Momma, and Papa too. And I have no doubt that you all will help me.

I will close for now. I just want that event to settle in your thoughts.

Thank you for surrounding me with such love.

I am forever in your debt,

A stronger Annie

CHAPTER 12 — MAY 17, 1947

Marie
How to Tie a Knot

TODAY IS THE DAY!

Al and I decided to go ahead and tie the knot. We have been together for more than a year. There really is nothing standing in our way. He has a good job, and although I have not finished college yet, I still have the money F-D-F gave me.

There will be no wedding. That is a waste of money. We are going to the clerk of court's office and sign the papers. We decided to prepare some words to say to each other. I am practicing mine before we meet at the courthouse. Suzy is in town to stand with me. We need a witness and what better one than my sister. Mom and N-D-L know marriage is important to me and Al, but they don't know we are doing it today. She is gonna be as mad as a wet hen. She also will be fuming about Suzy not telling her. But she will get over it. She always does sooner or later.

I didn't go home right after the semester ended

this year. Al and I were planning ahead. Since we'd be moving into the small house he'd found, it didn't seem to make sense for me to pack up and move twice. I've been setting up house for two weeks. He was still staying at the boarding house he had been in for the last year and coming by most evenings after work to help. We painted the inside all white. That was practical, he said. Even though I wanted a celery green bedroom, he said we'd buy that paint color when we bought our own house. After the painting was done, I finished organizing what furnishings we had, which was not much. Suzy had packed the car with my stuff from our shared bedroom at home. "Momma and N-D-L were too busy to notice," she said, "so all's clear."

Al brought the rest of his stuff over this morning. Hopefully I will get that all sorted before we go to the courthouse. Suzy and I will meet him there at two o'clock. When Al and I return, I want him to see everything arranged just like the home of a married couple.

I practiced my lines once more in front of Suzy. I wanted to know them well enough not to need to read them. She objected. "Those are nice things to say, Marie, but I don't see the point. Let's just get the clerk to sign the papers and get the heck outta there. It's not like it's a real wedding."

Not sure who I was trying to convince, I replied, "I know it is not a wedding, but it is a special moment in our life, and we need to show each other why we are getting married. Otherwise it's just a legal transaction."

"Well, isn't that what it is? There is no preacher

blessing the marriage. And no parents wishing you well. I still think it is the wrong idea. But you are my sister, and I am doing this for you. Momma is gonna send me away for life for not telling her about this. You owe me big time!"

I sat down with Suzy and grabbed her hands. I said, "I know how you feel about this. And I appreciate you for doing it anyway. Arguing about it today will not change anything that is happening. Momma will not blame you. Well, maybe just a little. But she knows I am as hard headed as she is and when I decide something, I follow through with it. And I don't remember her having a wedding for any of her marriages!"

I went into the bedroom to get ready. This was the room that would be for the married couple. I combed my hair, and I put on my new dress. It was white seersucker fabric that fit snug and fell just above my knees. At the waist was a soft green satin belt. I pulled on my matching green shoes and went to the kitchen where Suzy was waiting. She pulled out her camera and said, "At least we ought to have pictures for Momma, Larry, and Frank. You look beautiful."

Suzy was my driver. It was the first time I had ridden in her new car. "What do you think, Marie? Do you like my Chevrolet? We've never had a Chevrolet in our family, but it is American made, so Larry approved. I bought it with my own money, kinda. I put down $100 and am making payments for the rest. Do you like it?"

"I like it, Suzy. It is beautiful inside and out. And my favorite kind of car is a two-door. It looks sportier than the family four-door style. Let's see what this baby can do on the road!"

With Suzy's fast driving, we arrived at the courthouse ten minutes early, and there was Al standing outside. I like that he is punctual. And I also really liked how he looked. His reddish hair was carefully combed to one side. I love that man's hair. I had run my hands through it enough to know how soft it is. Ooh la la. He wore a black suit with a white shirt and green tie. The color of the tie was exactly the same as my belt. "Look at that tie, Suzy. How did he know?"

She just smiled back at me. Now I knew. I hope it was his idea to match the tie rather than Suzy's insistence.

I walked toward him. With that cock of the head and the wink of an eye, Al whistled and crooned, "Wowsa, Marie. You look so good. I guess this means we are still doing this. I am the luckiest fella in the world right now."

He knew how to turn a girl's head. I saw that from the first time I met him at that dance a year ago. I am glad I was always his last dance. "Yes, we are doing this, Mr. Roberts. Let's get a move on! By the way, you're lookin' pretty hot yourself."

There were three other couples waiting inside the assigned courtroom. The long narrow aisle led to a judge's desk. I could see a jury box on the right and the attorneys' desks in front of the bar. I was jarred a bit with the irony of a courtroom where people are judged innocent or guilty used as a place to get married and start a new life.

Suzy walked in first. I was holding Al's hand when

we entered. Al tapped Suzy on the shoulder and leaned forward, "I can't wait to be your brother, little lady."

"Brother-in-law," she quickly replied.

After another step Suzy stopped and faced Al. We almost crashed into each other. She looked right in Al's eyes and spoke to him in a way that unsettled me but also made me love her even more. "Al Roberts, before we do this, let me set the record straight. You are Marie's chosen fella, but if you ever hurt her or stop loving her, the entire Nash family will unchoose you the hard way. You got that?"

Startled he responded, "Geez, Suzy, yeah. I got that."

I interjected, "Move on, Suzy. I want to marry this man."

Thirty minutes later we were standing in front of the man who would pronounce us husband and wife. Suzy stood so close to me I could hear her breathing. Al placed his hand in mine and kissed my cheek. The clerk reminded him of the procedure, "Whoa. Slow down, sir. We are not to the kissing part yet." He looked at Suzy and said, "Do you solemnly witness this marriage between," he paused to look at a sheet of paper, "between Marie Frances Nash and Albert James Roberts?"

"Yes, I do," Suzy replied.

Whew, I thought, that was one hurdle we cleared. Suzy must have known what I was thinking. She nudged me with her right elbow and flashed a smile at me.

"Marie and Albert, have you prepared words for this time?"

With a look of frustration, Al looked at the clerk and said, "My name is Al. And yes, I want to say these words to Marie."

Al reached into his trouser pocket and pulled out a folded and dog-eared piece of paper. He read from it. "I, Al James Roberts with Suzy Dixon Nash as my witness, do take you, Marie, to be my lawful wedded wife to have and to hold, from this day forward, for better, for worse, for richer, for poorer, in sickness and in health, to love and to cherish, till death do us part."

He leaned over to me and whispered, "I found that in a book. Snazzy, huh?"

I loved that man so much right then. That was just like it would be if we were married in the church with my family around me. I kissed him on the cheek and said, "You did good, Albert." I looked at the clerk expecting him to admonish me for the kiss. He did not.

I straightened my shoulders, faced Al and said the words I had written. "Al James Roberts, I want to be your wife and you to be my husband. I will love you and want to be loved by you in sickness and in health and in happiness and sadness. I want us to cherish and respect each other for all the days of our lives."

The clerk nodded and looked back at Al and said, "If you have a ring, please gift it now."

We both had a gold band for the other. We exchanged them, saying just a simple "I love you" to each other.

The clerk addressed the whole room, now with only three people in it besides him, "By exchanging rings, you are consenting to be bound together as husband and wife. You are promising to honor, love, and support each other for the rest of your lives. By the authority vested in me by the laws of the State of North Carolina, I now pronounce you husband and wife."

Al planted a really good kiss on my lips. I wished I could hear wedding music being played. I wished my momma, Larry, and Frank were here. I hope I won't be sorry we did it like this.

Yelling, "Yahoo," Al picked me up and carried me all the way down the aisle and out the door. When we got into the street, he shouted to no one and everyone, "Hello, world! I just married the best girl on earth!"

Suzy and I were both laughing. "No regrets," I said to myself.

We hurried to Al's car as if it was urgent that we get this new life started. There were beer cans tied to the bumper and words written with shaving cream on the boot. I laughed. There was the proof.

AL AND MARIE MAN AND WIFE

"My buddies did this. Ain't it great?" Al looked around as if to see them nearby. No one we knew was there. Then we dashed around to the passenger side of the car. There were green ribbons tied to the car handle. Al pulled them loose, tossed one to Suzy and tied another in my hair. He swung open the door, bowed, and motioned for me to enter.

Suzy ran up before I sat down and gave me a big hug. She demanded, "Be happy, Marie! Happiness doesn't come easy—but it is worth it. I love you so much!" She stood up and gave Al a peck on the cheek. She whispered something to him that I couldn't hear. No doubt it was some kind of warning.

Driving away from the courthouse, I scooted over near him and leaned my head on his shoulder. I felt blissful and content at the same time. "Mr. Roberts, take me to our home where we will make a life together."

I was giddy when we drove up to the house. It all felt new and wonderful. Al opened my car door and announced, "Mrs. Roberts, let's go see this home. I can't wait to live with you—all the days of my life."

I marched formally to the door, swung open the screen door, and handed him the key. He held it up and looked at it as if it was gold. He planted a kiss on the key and put it in the lock. He threw open the door. Momma, Larry, Suzy, and Frank were standing there. They all shouted, "Congratulations!" and tossed yellow rose petals at us.

Al picked me up, carried me in, and placed me down in front of my momma. We just stood facing each other. She stood on her tip toes and pulled me to her. It was a silent hug between mother and daughter. Pulling back from her, I looked at her face covered in tears.

"Marie, I am happy for you. But don't you ever leave me out of something wonderful in your life again! You hear?"

Then I began to shed happy tears. "Yes ma'am. Never again."

Larry stepped over and joined the hug. "Me neither, Marie. Don't leave me out, ever. I can help buffer your mother." Momma and I giggled through our tears.

I went to Suzy, "Did you do this? Did you lie to me about keeping our secret?"

She smiled and nodded, "Heck yeah, I did. You were making a big mistake doing this without the Nash family around."

The only reply I could make was a thank you hug.

Al was talking to everyone. He must have been in on it the way he was acting. Al was as happy as I hoped he would be. I hope our marriage is like this always. But happiness does not always hang around. Sometimes we have to go look for it.

There was my first dad. Frank Pollard was standing on the other side of the room, watching me. I walked to him and said, "Thank you for coming. I wanted you to be part of this, but I didn't want a big wedding. It is perfect that you came."

He stroked my hair and looked at me with those blue eyes, the likeness that we shared. "Marie, finding a good partner is the best thing in the world. I am lucky to have had your momma so we could have you. Seeing you happy like this warms my heart. I have been waiting to see you begin your own family. Promise me that you will keep me close. You will have babies, and I want to know them. I want them to know their first grandpa."

"Of course. I would like that."

F-D-F walked over to Momma. He kissed her on the cheek and whispered in her ear. She looked at him as if years were melting away. Smoothing her skirt with her hands, she blushed. Taking a step back she replied, "You are welcome. It means so much to Marie that you are here. Me too, Frank."

Heading toward the kitchen of our little home, Momma hesitated. She turned to face us all and said, "My baby girl just got married. I hope she has found one that sticks with her and that she can forgive when he makes mistakes."

Suzy brought in a tray of cups filled with pink punch for everyone. As she passed them around, she shouted, "Amen, Momma! Let's drink to forgiveness!"

As dark was approaching, Larry announced that it was time to leave. "Ok, guys and dolls, let's get outta here. Al and Marie need some alone time." He winked at Al.

I grabbed Al's hand and said to the crowd, "I want you to know how much this meant to me. I am sorry for sneaking this in, but we didn't want to cause any expense. We just wanted to make it all official. I wish Caroline and Annie and her family could be here, then I would have all the people I love in the whole world in my parlor."

Al held up his cup, agreeing with Larry's suggestion, "Yes. We thank you for coming." He visibly yawned. I shoved him a bit with my shoulder but did not protest. Everyone laughed and started gathering their things.

After saying goodbye to everyone, Al went to the kitchen. I began picking up when I heard the POP of a champagne bottle. He joined me in the parlor carrying the bottle and two beautiful glasses I had never seen before. "I bought these glasses a few weeks ago. They are crystal and cost a pretty penny. I wanted us to have something really special every time we wanted to celebrate."

I held the glasses. He filled them with pizazz holding the bottle top near the glass rim and raising it way above our faces. The liquid flowed in smoothly then magically turned into bubbles that looked like diamonds. How glorious!

He tipped his glass toward me and said, "Marie, thank you for marrying me."

I nodded with my full glass and said, "And thank you for loving me enough to marry me." We kissed. It felt more significant than it ever had before. Al put his arm around me as we strolled 20 steps to the bedroom.

I giggled. "I love our little house," I said. "It takes us no time to get from room to room."

We both fell on the bed loving each other. Before dawn we were husband and wife in the eyes of God.

~~~

After what felt like hours of the best sleep I'd ever had, I left the bedroom quietly. Al was sleeping so deeply; I could hear his heavy breathing. He must be as content as I am.

I went to the kitchen to find exactly what I was looking for. In the top cabinet above the refrigerator was the box. A box so full of memories it seemed to weigh ten pounds. The outside of this Hav-a-Tampa box was designed to look like it was made of wood. The words Havatampa Cigar Co. Made in Tampa were ironic. This was passed down from grandma's house to

Aunt Dianne then to Momma, and now to me. I never
knew anyone in my grandma Flo's house to ever smoke
a cigar. Nor had anyone ever talked about going to
Tampa.

I set the sturdy paper box on our small kitchen
table and pulled out the contents. There was a pile of
letters. There were photographs and mementos, and
there was an envelope stuffed with important papers.
I went to my pocketbook to retrieve our marriage
license. This is the place it should be. In with all the
other reminders of who I am.

I decided to brew some coffee and reminisce.

Among the photographs were portraits of my
mother, her three sisters, and a picture of Suzy and
me when we were young. Those Nash sisters were very
close, and they still are. Many things have changed in
their lives, but they have stuck it out—together.

I pulled out a necklace that Frank gave me the day
we first met. I was a teenager. Momma has never seen
it. She didn't want me to know Frank, especially as my
dad by birth. I was thirteen before she told me I had
a father before George. George had always been my
papa. He was the best father a girl could have. I miss
him to this day. This heart-shaped necklace reminds
me that people belong to families in all different ways.
I clasped it around my neck for the very first time.

I put my hand on a folded peace crane. Suzy and
I made them as her momma lay sick in her bed. We
were trying to feel better by doing something for others.
We folded peace cranes for the soldiers fighting in the
war. We wanted the men fighting for our country to

know we cared. Momma promised to get them to the candy company that would mail them oversees with their boxes of candy. I think Suzy and I folded 25 cranes that day. We wrote sayings on the cranes, some to make us laugh, some words of encouragement. This one says *Twinkies for Pigs* on one side and *Come Home Safe* on the other. It was a copy of one that we sent. The soldiers would never know our real Twinkies story, but we knew the words would make them smile.

After emptying the box, I saw what I had written on the bottom. *Suzy Got Adopted June 9, 1940.* I was overwhelmed with love for my sister. That was the day Momma and Papa told Suzy that her mother, my Aunt Dianne, had arranged for her to live with us. Suzy's momma died that night as if now was a good time since that was organized. It was a very happy/sad day for me. Suzy was my best friend and now my sister.

I put the marriage license in the envelope with my birth certificate. That seems to sum it up. When I finish my degree, I will put that diploma in here too.

I decided not to re-read the letters. Doing that might make me cry. Today is the first day of my marriage. It is a happy day. These were letters Momma wrote to me when she was away. Most of these are about Aunt Caroline. Momma was good at reporting details, at least as much as I could handle.

Among the letter collection, there is one written to me before I was old enough to understand. It may be my favorite. Momma had gone to visit her sister Dianne in a hospital. Momma spent several days there while Aunt Dianne recovered. Although the letter talks about some medical details of Dianne's fall and the damage to her skull, Momma mostly told me a story of love in that letter.

I couldn't resist. I opened that letter penned by Momma in October 1935. The paper had darkened over time, the creases made the paper thin, and each page was dog-eared from me reading it so many times. Now might just be the perfect time to re-visit this.

My sweet Marie,

I know you are only seven and will not be able to understand what is in this letter now. I still want to write it so I won't forget what happened to Dianne. When you are older, I'll give you all the letters I write about my experiences. Heck, maybe someday they will be a book.

Some of the best conversations happen while waiting at the hospital or spending time with people who need companionship for long periods of time. In these times, topics do not end. They move into the next subject and then it comes back to what you were talking about earlier. This cycle of conversation happens over and over like bees flying from flower to flower, collecting more nectar. All this talking and listening spreads out into what else you remember. Shared memories uncover new views. That's how you begin to really understand. Marie, as you grow, take advantage of these moments. Make the time for conversations in waiting times.

This happened when spending time with Dianne after she took that bad fall. After she called out for a while, one neighbor finally heard her and found her. Other neighbors got her to the hospital. Another neighbor sent a telegram to me and George right away. Dianne had been in the hospital a full day before I could get to her.

I couldn't believe what I saw when I entered her hospital room (with nine other beds full of people). She looked like she'd been beaten by the mob. Dianne broke her leg and crashed her skull open by falling off the cement porch. By the time I saw her, the leg was wrapped from hip to heel. A bandage was wrapped all around her head, covering her forehead and just above the ears. She had small bandages on elbows, one hand, and around her ribs. Her face was black and blue. Over the next few days, her bruises turned yellowish. Just like when any wound heals, it gets harder and harder to see. That is true of physical wounds and mental ones.

I was scared for Dianne, not because she had broken bones, cuts, and scrapes, but because she loves her dead husband so much that she wants to be with him. I don't believe you should ever love someone more than yourself. If they leave or die, you must go on.

The reason Dianne fell was she kept seeing Joe in her mind. By the time you read this, Marie, you will know that Joe died the year before in a work accident.

She never really got over losing him. I knew that, but I didn't know she talked to him most days. I told her how foolish she was to do that. She said talking to Joe helped her get through it. If he didn't come see her from heaven, she would not have been able to live to take care of Suzy.

She whispered, "I feel like I have nobody who really understands. I love him so much. And he loves me. He took care of me. He respected me. Joe was a part of me. After he died, I realized if I didn't keep him in my brain, my brain would shrink. My heart would crack. I would never fully recover."

Marie, the day she fell, she had seen him in the backyard looking at her. Dianne said, "He summoned me to be with him. Right then I felt such peace and warmth. I knew what I should do. I ran to him. All I wanted was to be with him."

Dianne tripped, fell on the cement, broke her leg, cracked her skull, and nearly bled to death.

Marie, I've never known this kind of feeling. Of course, I know love, but not a kind of love that erases me. I believe love between a man and a woman should bring happiness and strength to get through the hard times. But it must not be the kind of dependence that you cannot survive without each other. We must all survive. And we will. We have sisters, children, and parents to worry about. We just can't will ourselves to die because life is hard.

I love your papa George. He is a good man, a good companion, and such a big help. George is my champion, as I am his. He is responsible to and for me. I am also responsible to and for him. He and I know each of us can exist without the other. We are individual people first, a couple second.

Dianne feels differently, and I didn't know that until we talked so many days in the hospital. I now understand her better. She will never change. I realize I need to stay close enough to be there for her when the sadness takes over and she can't find happiness. After coming home from that visit with Dianne, I talked with George about all of it. He and I agreed we needed to move to Burlington to be close to Dianne.

Marie, you will fall in love many times. You will someday think that one of them is the one for a lifetime. I'll be happy for you – if I like him. But please remember what I learned. Love does not keep you alive. Your strength to find happiness keeps you alive.

The best kind of love comes from your momma anyway.

Momma

I put down the letter and looked toward the closed bedroom door. I want all the love Momma had with George and the kind she has now with Larry. And I wouldn't mind having a little of the kind that she and Frank had together.

Does Al want the same kind of love that I do? We may not know that now, but we have a lifetime to find out what love means to us. It will take lots of conversation to understand each other. I think I'll go back to the bed now, so we can begin.

About the Author

Leatha Marie's career has been focused with and around children. She taught public school in rural North Carolina where she learned the difference between street and book smarts—and the value of both. The majority of her career was in mentoring the next leaders in early childhood education corporations. All the while she gained stories of life, loyalty, and challenge, and how resilience leads to success. Lately, her work has involved coaching, writing, and training business managers to become more leader than boss.

Reading non-fiction books and articles has fed Leatha's talents. Reading fiction for pleasure has fed her soul. Writing personal journals has helped her capture the happiest and most impactful moments of life. Those journals hold tight her observations on what bonds or fractures relationships. Over the years, she has collected a marvelous assortment of characters, family, and friends who add narrative to her life.

Living in the South where many things "are not talked about" encouraged Leatha Marie to unearth what might really be happening. She has lived among a funny, sometimes outrageous, extended family that has blessed her with plenty of stories.

Leatha grew up in Raleigh, NC. She is a Meredith College graduate with a double major in History and Early Childhood Education and an MBA. *Happiness Doesn't Come Easily* is her second novel. Learn more about Leatha Marie and The Nash Sisters books at **LeathaMarie.writewaypublishingcompany.com.**

A Message from the Author

Dear Readers,

More of the Nash family journey is coming. The family has so much to say! Book number three in this series will be available in late 2021.

In the meantime, thank you for reading the stories I love to tell. If you have a few minutes, I would deeply appreciate a book review wherever you purchased this book. Reviews help other readers find books, and authors like me truly appreciate that!

Gratefully yours and until next time,
Leatha Marie

Made in the USA
Middletown, DE
14 April 2021